The Casebook of Inspector Armstrong

Volume III

Martin Daley

Paperback ISBN 978-1-78705-221-5
ePub ISBN 978-1-78705-222-2
PDF ISBN 978-1-78705-223-9

Published in the UK by MX Publishing
335 Princess Park Manor, Royal Drive,
London, N11 3GX
www.mxpublishing.co.uk

For Rodger and Jill

The Young American

June 1896

As a shaft of sunlight streamed into the carriage and the train rattled through northern Cumberland towards Carlisle, Professor Wilson peered expectantly out of the window. He was making a journey that he had been looking forward to since childhood, when his mother Janet regaled him with stories about the city where she was born.

Listening to his mother's recollections, it seemed to young Tommy – as his family called him – that this small, blackened industrial city in the north of England might as well be another planet from the sultry, tropical surroundings of his own birthplace in the Southeast of the United States.

Janet was one of eight children born to Minister Thomas Woodrow and his wife, Marion, prior to the family emigrating to America from Carlisle in 1835. In adulthood, Janet also married a minister, Joseph Wilson, who took up a position at the First Presbyterian Church in Staunton, Virginia in 1854.

It was here that the couple had four children; the third named after his maternal grandfather and nicknamed Tommy by his parents and older sisters. Born just prior to the disastrous Civil War, some of Tommy's earliest memories included watching his mother tending to Confederate soldiers in the local hospital. It was such acts of selflessness demonstrated by his parents during these formative years – amid the poverty-stricken and devastated

1

South – that nurtured Tommy's appreciation of family and heritage.

He was destined to demonstrate such values throughout his personal and professional life. He met his own future wife, Ellen, while studying history and politics at John Hopkins University in Baltimore; the two were married on the banks of the Savannah River in 1885.

The following five years saw the arrival of three daughters and the offer of a professorship at the College of New Jersey, all of which curtailed Wilson's ambition of crossing the Atlantic to visit his mother's birthplace.

That was until the unexpected sequence of events throughout the first half of the year 1896, which led to him sitting on the train anticipating its arrival at Carlisle.

The professor had been instrumental in working towards the college becoming a university for many months. His work culminated in university status being granted in the spring of 1896, and Princeton University was born. At the same time, the senior academic moved his family into a new larger house, as befitting a senior tutor from such an esteemed seat of learning.

The intense domestic and professional activity had taken its toll on the professor, and in May, he suffered a medical ailment for which his doctor advised a long vacation in order to recuperate.

Not only was Wilson a well-known, highly respected figure within the Princeton community, he and his family had clearly made a favourable impression with their wealthy, widowed neighbour Mrs. Brown. Upon hearing of Mr. Wilson's "mild stroke" as his doctor had termed it, and his suggested trip to recuperate, she offered to pay for a trip to England for him and Ellen. After Wilson's initial polite refusal of his neighbour's generous offer, Ellen persuaded her husband to go alone, in order that he could fulfil his long-held ambition, while she would stay at home with their daughters.

This placed him in a dilemma: a genuine wish to fulfil a lifetime's ambition, set against a feeling of guilt at having to leave his wife and daughters behind for two months. It was a decision the professor struggled with until the moment of no return, when he found himself in the bustling shipping office of New York Harbour in late May 1896.

Scores of people were squeezed into the office while hundreds more thronged the quayside, excitedly chattering and shouting over the sound of the gulls and ships' horns, in every language imaginable. In the crowd, Wilson's shoulders were concertinaed as he grasped his luggage to his chest and was carried along, almost involuntarily through the office towards the counter, and the clerk whose deadpan expression seemed completely incongruous with the excitement and anticipation being demonstrated by everyone else.

By the time he was shuffled forward, the professor knew that neither the surly character across the desk from him, nor the mass of impatient people behind him would tolerate a discussion about his uncertainty about the journey. So when his turn came the Princeton man simply said the official, "Good afternoon, I have a reservation for the *Ethopia* to Glasgow, Scotland." He gave the man his name and within the hour Professor Wilson was crossing one of the huge gangplanks that connected the trans-Atlantic vessel with the dockside.

Three days out from New York: Wilson was out on deck on a beautiful sunny afternoon reading a history of the area he was about to visit, when a couple who were out strolling asked if they could take the two vacant chairs that were beside him. He acquiesced with a gesture of invitation and put his book down out of politeness.

Responding to the gesture, the man offered his hand, "Charles Wood and my wife, Elizabeth," he said. He explained that they were planning a cycling tour of Scotland and England.

"What a coincidence," said Wilson with a smile, "I'm also intending to cycle throughout the Lake District of England.

"It sure is a small world!" exclaimed Wood. He told the professor that he was a banker in New York but he and his wife originated from Windermere, Florida. "It was a bit of a whim a couple of years ago when we thought it would be neat to visit the original Windermere in Cumberland, England."

"We instantly fell in the love with the area," continued Elizabeth. "So this time we plan to spend a little more time there, but first we want to visit the Highlands of Scotland which we hear is just as beautiful."

The three spent several hours over the next couple of days getting to know one another and discussing their plans for the two months ahead. They agreed to meet up and cycle together in the Lakes. "Last time we stayed at the George Hotel in a town called Penrith just north of the Lake Ullswater," said Wood, "Why don't we meet there?"

"When would be good for you, Mr. Wilson?" asked Elizabeth.

The professor had some university business to attend to in both Edinburgh and Cambridge before he commenced his holiday proper, so he consulted his diary. "What better date than the 4th of July!" he said.

*

After the long journey, Professor Wilson was now finally here in the city where his mother was born. He had gorged on the city's history in preparation for his trip: its association with Kings and Queens of both England and Scotland, who appeared to have wrestled for control of the border city for centuries since the Romans first established a settlement there two thousand years earlier.

As he had explained to Mr. and Mrs. Wood on the crossing, particular highlights he was looking forward to were visiting Cockermouth and Grasmere, both synonymous with one of his literary heroes, William Wordsworth.

Stepping down from the train, the platform was a hive of activity with both station staff and passengers who jostled each other in their haste, regardless of whether they were arriving or departing.

A phalanx of porters appeared, seemingly from nowhere, to help with carrying luggage. One approached the American visitor and offered to take his bags. Having just a light rucksack and one carpet bag, Wilson was about to politely refuse the service; that was until he gripped the handle of the carpet bag and was instantly reminded of the slight debilitation he suffered in his right hand as a result of his medical scare the previous month.

"Thank you that would be really kind," he said whilst retrieving a piece of paper from the top pocket of his traveling jacket. "I assume we haven't far to go the Station Hotel, but it's been a long journey, and I would appreciate the hand."

"No problem sir," said the porter shouldering the rucksack and picking up the bag, "your hotel is just outside; I'll show you the way."

At the entrance to the station, the visitor paused to savour his first impression. The pretty cobbled square with its gently sloping contours was peppered with pedestrians and barrow-boys, shuttling their goods to and from the trains. A line of hansom cabs and four wheelers stood ready to carry arrivals to their destination in and around the city; the cabbies shouting their conversation with one another over the sound of their restive horses.

Dominating the immediate skyline were the imposing, twin drum towers that the visitor read had been built in the sixteenth century to improve the city's defences and now appeared to create a natural entrance to the city.

"Sir?" the porter disturbed the tourist's smiling reverie.

"Oh yes, I'm sorry," replied Wilson.

"The hotel is just here on the right, sir."

The two climbed the few steps up to the main entrance and the tourist tipped the porter as he set his bags down in the foyer. "That's very kind sir, thank you," said the latter touching the brim of his cap before returning the few yards to the station and his next task.

A middle-aged man appeared from behind a screen to the rear of the front desk. "Good afternoon sir, can I help you?"

The guest's attention was taken by a portrait of Queen Victoria that hung behind the desk. "I see I'm in good company," he said to the hotelier with an indicating nod and a smile.

"The man looked behind him, "Yes sir, Her Majesty has stayed here on her way to Balmoral on more than one occasion." Then turning back to his guest he asked, "Do you have a reservation sir?"

"Yes, I do," he replied, "I'm here for three nights initially, and then I will be returning for a further two nights in three weeks' time."

"What name is it sir?" asked the hotelier running his finger down the ledger that lay before him.

"Woodrow Wilson," said the man.

Empty

"There's been another one, sir."

Inspector Cornelius Armstrong was sitting at his desk, deep in thought, twisting the horns of his moustache, when he looked up to see Sergeant Bill Townsend filling the doorway of his office.

"Is it at Stanwix again?" he asked, immediately aware of what the sergeant was referring to.

"No, Dalston Road this time," said Townsend.

Armstrong looked down at the plan of Stanwix Cemetery that lay on his desk and absentmindedly tapped the plot marked with an X.

Two years ago, almost to the day – and a few days before his thirtieth birthday – he had become the youngest Detective Inspector in the City Police's history. When the old Chief Constable retired, and Armstrong's friend and mentor Henry Baker assumed the top job, the latter had no hesitation in promoting the young man to his former post.

It was a break in tradition and a decision that raised a few eyebrows amongst local officialdom. A small, regional constabulary like Carlisle usually adopted a promotional system that was based on seniority and waiting for dead-men's-shoes, as exemplified by the other Detective Inspector Godfrey Parker, someone whom Baker had carried for years. It was rather taken for granted that in a small regional force, if called for, its senior officers would combine their detective work with ordinary policing but Parker had developed a technique that saw him virtually avoid all aspects of police work. It wasn't that he was particularly lazy; his natural dithering manner meant he was regularly overtaken by his younger colleagues who – given that he was the most senior serving policeman – viewed him as a gentle, mild-mannered and kindly old man for whom they were happy to make allowances.

The one incident that summed up Parker took place when he was still a uniformed officer some thirty years earlier; despite the fact that none of his current colleagues were part of the force at the time, they were the latest generation to snigger at the thought of poor Parker being outwitted by a thief who was locked in the cells at the back of the station. He shouted down the corridor to Godfrey Parker who was the only officer on duty during the late afternoon, complaining about the smell coming from the drains in his cell. When Parker opened the cell and entered to investigate, he was overpowered by the villain who let himself out, and locked the policeman in behind him. The thief made his escape and was never seen again. It was the first incident of many that Parker became famed for during his stumbling career.

"I need someone I know and can trust, Cornelius," said Henry Baker to his young protégé, when he assumed the chief constable role. His proposal took Armstrong completely by surprise. "Dear old Godfrey has been winding down for retirement ever since I joined the City Force twenty years ago."

After a bit of persuasion and much thought, Cornelius accepted Henry's offer, and now, two years on, he had justified Baker's decision and built a reputation as being the best officer on the local force; one to whom everyone –

including at times his superior officer – would go with a problem.

Armstrong had a presence about him that seemed to set him aside from the others; with his dapper appearance and apparent self-assuredness, he commanded unanimous respect from all of his colleagues, despite the majority of them being senior to him both in terms of age and length of service.

Yet for all his success and the respect others naturally afforded him, Cornelius was still prone to spells of self-doubt, whenever an answer didn't come to him quickly; wondering if he were up to the job and continually concerned about letting people down – the same people who just assumed that he would solve the case at hand. He felt the first indications of such a feeling as he sat tapping the plan that lay on the desk in front of him.

"Brady and Gibson were in the area when the alarm was raised about an hour ago," said Townsend, breaking the detective's absentmindedness, "they're up there at the cemetery now."

The station was relatively quiet: a couple of bobbies were sitting in the arear behind the front desk writing reports on incidents they had attended respectively the previous day, while a woman, wrapped in a woollen shawl and wearing a modest bonnet sat patiently in the waiting area to speak with the desk sergeant.

Armstrong had been at his desk for less than twenty minutes reading what little information was available regarding the disturbance of a grave in the Stanwix Cemetery two nights earlier. Now he slowly took his jacket off the hook and slipped his arms into it, then he levered himself into his knee length overcoat and put on his bowler. He began to fear that what he initially thought was a distasteful, isolated incident, could now possibly develop into a series of body snatching episodes that were so commonplace in the early nineteenth century.

A keen student of local history, Cornelius was aware that his home city had not been exempt from the gruesome crimes that were more readily associated with the likes of Edinburgh and London. With this in mind he instructed Townsend, "Get me any information you can on the grave robbing incidents of about sixty or seventy years ago. There should be something in the old ledgers in the back room. Failing that, speak with the librarian Sydney Irvine at Tullie House – he will have the old newspapers of the day."

He then instructed PC Harry Stokes – one of the report-writing constables – to get the horse-drawn police wagon and take him to Carlisle Cemetery, situated on the edge of the city on Dalston Road.

*

"Got a good day for it sir," commented Stokes ironically, as he and his superior rattled along Shaddongate towards Dalston Road. It had rained quite heavily through the night and the grey clouds remained over the city. "Sun never shines at funerals," added the uniformed officer.

Cornelius gave him a sideways glance and shook his head quietly, "You should have been a philosopher Harry."

As Stokes drove under the arched entrance of the cemetery, it was immediately apparent where the desecration had taken place. Two hundred yards ahead on the right, in the paupers' burial ground, a clutch of people had gathered. Necks strained, elbows nudged, and no doubt tongues wagged; the usual group of voyeurs and snoops were drawn like magnets towards misfortune or wrongdoing.

They were being marshalled by the two uniformed officers Townsend had referred to. Much to his chagrin Armstrong also saw Jack Dixon from the Carlisle Journal there, no doubt keen to trample on someone's feelings to get a story. Inevitably, it was Dixon who addressed the inspector as he climbed down.

"What d'you think, Inspector, are Burke and Hare back on the scene?"

The desultory chatter of the onlookers gave way to sniggers at the reporter's interruption.

"I think we should have a little more respect for the situation," said Armstrong, and then addressing the crowd through his constables, "Let's clear this area."

Gibson and Brady immediately started shepherding the now compliant onlookers back to a respectable distance. "You too, sir," Gibson said to Dixon who was less eager to move back. Once the crowd had retreated toward the entrance of the cemetery, some lost interest in the potential scandal and, with their mawkish curiosity satisfied, started to drift away.

Armstrong watched as the two constables returned to the graveside. They were followed by a man who emerged from the office beside the main entrance; he wore a black frock coat and a sombre expression. His awkward gait was compounded by his attempt to hurry along whilst balancing an opened leather bound ledger on one forearm and trying to steady it with his other hand.

As Gibson and Brady reached the graveside, the man had virtually caught them up. "Ah, Mr. East," said Gibson, turning to discover the man behind him, "let me introduce to you Inspector Armstrong, who is investigating the matter." And then turning to his superior "Sir, this is Mr. East, the cemetery manager. I asked him to establish whose grave it was."

"Good morning, Mr. East," said the inspector, half nodding and half inviting comment.

"Oh, a terrible business," said East, almost to himself, "a terrible business. Nothing like this has ever happened before. We always pride ourselves on having an immaculate facility where the deceased rest in peace and their relatives can come and find some comfort in this pleasant environment."

"The grave?" prompted Armstrong, eager to bring the manager back to the matter at hand.

"Oh yes," said East, regaining a little composure. He ran his finger down and then across the page of the ledger. "The grave contained the body of one Elizabeth Meggs, a pauper from the workhouse who died on the 20th of January 1833."

Cornelius looked into the dark gaping cavity: it was empty.

East followed his gaze, "The burial appears to have been typical of the day. The body would have been wrapped in a hessian shroud and would have been covered in lime before the grave was filled in."

Armstrong appeared to not hear: *Why would someone be digging into graves that were over seventy years old?* Something then caught his eye a couple of yards to the left of the grave. "What's that?" he asked, pointing to what looked like a stone that had been painted red, although the paint had faded considerably.

"It's a mark," said East. "It means that this area has been desecrated before."

"You mean other graves have been raided?"

"Yes, although not in my time here." He consulted the ledger again. "Yes, here: that grave appears to have been disturbed also in 1833. I seem to recall reading somewhere that there was a spate of body snatching around that time." He looked again and added as an afterthought, "Elsie Grimes – coincidentally, both she and Elizabeth Meggs were buried at six o'clock in the morning on the same day."

Armstrong stared into the middle distance as his thoughts reverted to Stanwix Cemetery across the river on the north side of the city. *I'm sure Stanwix was also involved in the grave robbing incidents.* As bizarre as it seemed, his instinct suggested it was worth eliminating any connection between the recent grave disturbances and the incidents that took place several decades earlier.

The Inspector addressed PC Stokes, "Harry, take Brady and the wagon and get yourselves up to Stanwix and double check the site of the disturbance up there," and then pointing to the worn stone, "see if there are any of these painted stones in the surrounding area."

He thanked Mr. East for his help and informed him that he might need to visit him again. He then informed his remaining officer, Gibson, that he would walk back to the station and asked him to remain on site until the last of the ghoulish spectators had finally dispersed.

A helpful acquaintance

How would anyone know which graves to rob given that they were so old? Surely it couldn't be coincidence that the Meggs' grave was right next to the Grimes' grave that was disturbed all those years ago? Perhaps the robbers were particularly looking for the red stones to signify the original desecration? But then how would they would ever be able to pick them out under the cover of darkness? And what could they possibly do with a seventy year old skeleton? The whole reason for body snatching was to sell the corpses for dissection while they were still intact.

Armstrong's mind tied itself in knots as one unanswerable question usurped the last. *The whole thing just doesn't make sense,* he continually told himself as he walked back down Dalston Road towards Shaddongate.

He was experiencing the initial, confusing opening phase of any investigation. The amount – or in some cases, the lack of amount – of information, not to mention its complexity often gave the inspector a sense of being overwhelmed. Somehow he managed to keep such insecurities to himself, hiding what he saw as a weakness. Much of his investigative practice relied upon simply sitting quietly, either in his office or his sitting room and reflecting on the evidence that was available to him. What he didn't comprehend was that most of those around him, most notably Chief Constable Henry Baker, saw this as a level-headed strength, not a weakness.

But at this moment he was currently going through that initial, infuriating period: what little information was available was just washing over him not making much sense. If his emotional demons were telling him this case was beyond his capabilities, his inner logic re-assured him that his skills had gotten him this far in his career, and his tried and trusted methodology had proved in every case so far. *Hold your nerve and trust yourself!*

After giving himself a talking to and sifting out the nonsense, Cornelius decided to apply some old good fashioned common sense. In order to move equipment or a body, the robbers would need some form of transportation. As there was only one carter's yard between the city centre and the cemetery, it was possible that they had hired a vehicle in the days before.

Seth Graham had run his little carter's business in Shaddongate in the shadow of Dixon's Chimney for as long as Cornelius could remember. He had four carts of various sizes and six horses that he used personally, when commissioned to do so, but which he also hired out to anyone who needed something shifted. The one regular arrangement he had was with Gilly Millholme, the rag-and-bone man who had a horse and cart on regular hire.

When Armstrong joined the police, Seth's was one of the places he felt somehow protective of and would keep a close eye on as a result, as he patrolled the Caldewgate and Shaddongate areas, regularly calling in for a cuppa and a chat.

Graham's establishment consisted of a reasonably sized yard at the end of which was a workshop-cum-storeroom-cum-house, where Seth did just about everything both domestically and professionally.

17

The dark clouds had cleared and the sun was starting to peep through by the time Inspector Armstrong walked through the large wooden gates of the carter's yard. The overnight rain had dried on the cobbled surface leaving it feeling grimy underfoot, while puddles that were coated with a greasy film dotted the uneven yard. Adjacent to the gates on one side were two four-wheeled wooden carts; while on the opposite side was a large pile of horse manure that steamed away gently.

The owner was grooming two of his horses across the yard at the side of the building. It was an ironic trait of Seth Graham that he kept his horses in the best possible condition and appearance, while he neglected his own lamentably. One of his animals stood nibbling on a pile of hay while Seth was putting his back into brushing the hind quarters of its stable mate like a trainer preparing his steed for a prize race. Unlike their owner both animals looked happy and healthy.

Seth's habits and appearance had never altered in all the time Cornelius had known him. He wore a woollen shirt over which hung a misshapen, holed pullover and a battered sleeveless farrier's jacket. His scuffed hobnailed boots and colourless denim trousers were partially covered by knee-high leather gaiters, while on his head was a round, skull-hugging hat with a narrow down-brim that seemed to be suitable for all weathers. The only variation to this attire was when the carter wore a long oilskin during times of heavy rain.

A rolled up cigarette was never far from his lips, the result of which inflicted on him a wickedly raking cough; this along with his generally scruffy appearance and his permanently bristled chin, it was difficult to put an age on him. Those who knew him believed he must be well into his sixties, but then he had looked exactly the same for decades so no one was ever quite sure.

The policeman walked into the yard just as the carter hocked up a throat-full of phlegm and gobbed it out of harm's way. "Morning Seth," Cornelius called, "keeping healthy as ever, I see."

"Oh, hello Mr. Armstrong, long time, no see," replied Seth as he broke off from brushing the horse and instinctively gave it an affectionate slap on the rump.

He had known Cornelius for years, and was always comfortably on first-name terms with him throughout his uniform days, but ever since the latter's promotion to detective inspector, Seth had thereafter always used the formal title when addressing him, as if conscious of the hierarchal pecking order demanded by society. Cornelius had long since given up trying to assure the carter that it wasn't necessary and had resigned himself to them both playing out their respective roles in the social order.

After the usual, *how've you been keeping?* and *what's the latest?* small talk, the inspector outlined the purpose of his visit while trying to be as discreet about the case as possible.

"I'm looking into a particularly difficult matter at the moment, Seth, and I was wondering if you could indirectly help me. How's business been lately?"

The carter was a bit puzzled by the question but answered, "Yes, I've been really busy lately, Mr. Armstrong. Had a few jobs here and there – can't complain y'know."

"Have you had anyone actually hire a cart from you recently?"

"Yes, there's been three or four jobs in the last week or so."

"Can you tell me who?"

Seth looked a little sheepish, "Well, I've not been as good at keeping the books since the missus died a couple of years ago," he said.

Armstrong was sympathetic towards the elderly man but was keen to establish any possible areas of enquiry. "It could be important Seth. I'm looking for strangers or an unusual hiring."

"Follow me into the back," said the carter gesturing, "There should be something through there."

They went through the open doorway into the building. There were several wooden-spoked wheels leaning against the damp, bare-bricked walls, while three large barrels acted as pedestals for boxes and crates that were piled high to the ceiling. The two went through a further door that led into the kitchen area of the dwelling quarters beyond the workshop.

It had been a couple of years since Armstrong had been a guest of Seth Graham but the appearance and the smell of the kitchen hadn't changed. The comingled aroma of strong tea, wet washing and a permanently lit kitchen stove brought a half-smile to Cornelius's face.

"You sit down Mr. Armstrong and I'll make us a cup of tea."

The carter took a large two-handled tea pot and poured the black liquid into two tin mugs and slapped them down on the kitchen table. He then started sifting among some scraps of papers that were scattered on every available surface in his back kitchen.

"There was one that was a bit queer," he mumbled to himself. Finally retrieving the grubby piece of paper he was looking for, "Ah here it is. A bloke said he might need a cart for a week. Needed it to carry some tools, he said. Paid up front but then came back and said he didn't need it after all. Never asked for any money back – best job I ever had!"

"What was his name?" asked Cornelius.

Seth referred to the paper and squinted at his own appalling handwriting, "Gridley...Mr. Gridley, no first name. He said he was from Shropshire"

"Shropshire?" repeated Armstrong, "what's he doing up here?" he said, as much to himself as to Seth. Then recalling the nature of the crimes he was investigating, he realised the foolishness of his comment. *If they are stealing corpses, there is likely to be some out-of-town connection.*

"Was the man on his own?" he asked.

"He was," confirmed Seth, "although I seemed to remember he said something about his men." The carter thought for a while and then recalled, "That's it, I remember now! That's why he couldn't go ahead with the hire because his men weren't available all of a sudden. It all sounded a bit arse-about-face to me but, as I say, when he told me to keep the money for my trouble, I didn't ask any more questions."

The two continued to pass the time of day until Armstrong made his excuses and left the old man to his business. "You look after yourself Seth," he said as the two shook hands. He knew it was an instruction that would be ignored but made it anyway, keen as he was to let the old man know that he cared about his welfare.

On the way back to the station Armstrong pondered the morning's events and the strangely familiar name given to him by Seth Graham...*Mr. Gridley*

An unexpected visitor

Following his evening meal, Woodrow Wilson wrote his first letter home to Ellen telling her of his sea crossing, his encounter with Mr. and Mrs. Wood, and his safe arrival in Carlisle. For the first time in three weeks, he then enjoyed a stable night's sleep in a bed that remained motionless for eight glorious hours.

He rose refreshed and full of anticipation at the thought of exploring, during his first full day in the city. On the way back to his room following breakfast, he asked the desk clerk for directions to the various places he wished to visit and if there were a bicycle shop where he could hire a cycle for his touring in the Lakes. The professor couldn't help but smile at the man who – after describing each complex instruction – completed the direction by using the four words that everyone seems to use when giving directions to a stranger: "You can't miss it." He also informed him of Mr. Wheeler's Bicycle Shop on Abbey Street and suggested that the tourist couldn't miss it.

Wilson would proceed to spend most of the day trying to follow the clerk's various directions from a few notes he had scribbled down. Successes included his finding the house that his grandfather built for his family on Warwick Road; failures included his missing out on the chapel where the Reverend Woodrow preached, and the adjacent manse where his mother had been born.

It was market day and the city centre was a sea of humanity and noise. English Street was filled with stalls around which clattered the sound of hooves and wheels from omnibuses, carts and hansom cabs, while stall holders shouted above the din to be heard; all the while, the high pitched drone of a hurdy-gurdy floated around the square.

Woodrow enjoyed wandering around, soaking in such an atmosphere he had never witnessed before. Moreover, he realised he was also enjoying the anonymity afforded by his visit – being a well-known senior professor at Princeton, he would never be able to idly wander around so desultorily without being recognised and disturbed, however innocently or well-intended.

Picking his way through the stalls, Wilson found himself in front of the town hall, at the furthest end of English Street. By doing so he discovered the source of the music that contributed to the market scene. On a paved area in front stood the elderly musician, turning the crank of the hurdy-gurdy furiously. He was a sorry looking fellow who rocked uncomfortably from side to side between his one leg and the wooden stump that acted as a replacement for the other. He had straggly, greying hair which matched an unkempt beard, while a piece of thick string was tied round his middle, keeping his battered overcoat in place.

The tourist saw a coffee shop to the left of the town hall and decided it would be a good location to enjoy a light lunch, from where he could still enjoy the hubbub of the scene before him. He tossed a few coins into the hurdy-gurdy man's cap that lay on the ground in front of him – which prompted a toothless smile and salute from the unfortunate man – and headed towards the hostelry.

After his lunch he decided to visit the cathedral. The hotel clerk had given him directions to the bicycle shop that would take the visitor through the cathedral grounds onto

Abbey Street beyond, so Wilson thought it was natural to kill two birds with one stone, as it were, given that he intended to set off for the Lakes the following day.

After spending more than an hour walking around the cathedral, he left the grounds through the West Gate and found himself on Abbey Street. Wandering down the street he saw two men standing beside a cart upon which was lashed a large object covered with a tarpaulin. As he approached he was about to ask them if they knew where Mr. Wheeler's Bicycle Shop was, when he saw it immediately beyond them on the left.

He smiled and nodded at the men – who had started to untie the ropes of their cart, but who didn't seem in the best of moods – and made to enter the shop, only to find the "closed" sign on the door as he reached for the handle. He turned and was about to ask the men if they knew where the owner might be, or why his shop was closed, when he saw a smartly dressed gentleman walking along the street towards them.

*

It was mid-afternoon by the time Inspector Armstrong arrived back at the station. Walking had given him some reflection time. Initially he wondered if the original violation had been a sick prank but now that there had been a repeat within a couple of days, he could only conclude that there was more to it. Moreover, the fact that now the incidents were taking place on different sites, suggested that virtually all graveyards in the city were under threat.

There were always three constables carrying out a night beat around the city, and Armstrong was reluctant to pull them off their normal duties in order to guard the three main cemeteries at Dalston Road, Stanwix and Upperby. He therefore decided to get Sergeant Townsend to organise specific cover at the vulnerable sites. St. Cuthbert's Churchyard was also another possible target but as it was just a few hundred yards from the station on West Walls, Armstrong thought he could work a night shift himself and keep an eye on it, if he sent a uniformed officer to the other sites. Knowing his men as he did, Cornelius was mindful that such an act of leading by example would soften the blow of the unpopular order.

He checked in at the station and informed Sergeant Townsend of his plan. Townsend acknowledged the order and informed his superior that he had found a great deal of information about the body snatching incidents of the 1830s. It was half past three and Armstrong had a quick leaf through the pile of papers Townsend had gathered and decided there was a great deal of interest in them.

He informed the sergeant of his plans to return to his lodgings for some rest in preparation for his night shift at the station. "I'll go through them then," he said. "We'll then meet at eight o'clock tomorrow morning with the lads for a briefing," he added.

"Very good sir," said Townsend.

Cornelius ambled slowly along West Walls, towards his lodgings on nearby Abbey Street, deep in thought at this macabre puzzle and only vaguely cognisant of the distant sounds of the market on English Street that drifted through the lanes that linked the two main arteries.

He paused momentarily at the narrow junction of Heads Lane; glancing across at the top of the headstones in St. Cuthbert's that peeped over the walls of the churchyard, he wondered if they too were in danger of being defiled.

Wandering along Dean Tait's Lane and left onto Abbey Street, a wave of self-doubt washed over him. It was that self-doubt that made him such a good detective, his chief constable would often tell him.

He then saw an unusual scene a hundred yards ahead of him. Outside his lodgings stood an upright piano on the back of a wagon, with three men standing on the pavement, all of whom appeared to be in a state of some agitation. Cornelius suddenly remembered he had arranged for the piano to be delivered to his lodgings over two weeks ago, after purchasing it from Rattigan's Musical Instrument Shop on Botchergate.

He felt more than a little embarrassed by the triviality of the event given the subject that was now occupying his thoughts, but it was something he had arranged before the spate of grave-robbing started, and it was at a time when learning to play the piano seemed extremely important to the policeman. It had been an ambition of his since childhood and, having started to take lessons earlier in the year, taking receipt of his own instrument was something he was extremely excited about.

It was the latest luxury he had afforded himself since taking lodgings with Mrs. Wheeler two years earlier, following his promotion to inspector. He had received a modest education in childhood, but had resolved to educate himself in adulthood by expanding his reading of the classics and learning more about music. His landlady had agreed to him purchasing the piano on the condition that he didn't play it after eight in the evening.

Mrs. Wheeler's husband owned the bicycle shop immediately next door to number 22. The delivery men appeared to have suddenly realised that the piano was being delivered to *22a* – Cornelius's top floor rooms.

Two of the men were clearly there to do the heavy lifting judging by their build and attire but the third man looked distinct from the others. He was tall, bespectacled and wore clothes more in keeping with a tourist or a sportsman, than a workman. Cornelius wondered if he were there to supervise the delivery but when he spoke, it was clear that his presence outside his lodgings was purely coincidental.

As he approached, he addressed the two men who were waiting by the cart, "I'm really sorry lads, I forgot you were coming this afternoon." The men mumbled something about waiting, and the heavy task ahead of them.

Doffing his travelling cap and nodding towards the shop that was closed, the other man then spoke. "Good afternoon," he said, "you wouldn't be Mr. Wheeler by any chance would you?"

"No," replied Cornelius, "Thursday is half day closing and Mr. Wheeler and his wife always go to her sister's."

"That is unfortunate," said the man, "I am on vacation in the area and was hoping to hire a bicycle from his shop. I was told it was probably the best shop of its kind in the city."

Cornelius couldn't fail to notice the man's soft American accent. "That's true," he said, "although it's probably the only one of its kind" he added with a smile. "You sound as though you are a long way from home."

"Yes, in between researching my family history I'm hoping to do a little cycle touring. My name is Woodrow Wilson," he added offering a hand.

"Pleased to meet you Mr. Wilson," said the policeman in response the American's greeting, "I'm Cornelius Armstrong. I lodge at Mrs. Wheeler's" – he indicated the front door on his left; then referring to the cycle shop he continued, "Many shop keepers close when it's market day as takings are generally down."

"The bloody music shop doesn't though," interrupted one of the men impatiently.

"Sorry again, lads," said Armstrong, "maybe we could move this thing upstairs."

"I'm not sure if I would be of much use," said Wilson, "I recently had a problem with my arm, but I'm willing to give it a try."

"I didn't really mean you, Mr. Wilson," replied Cornelius, "but if you don't mind giving us a hand, I'm sure I can make you a cup of coffee while you wait for Mr. Wheeler's return. They normally return around five o'clock."

"That's a splendid idea," agreed the visitor.

"*Splendid,*" mumbled one of the workmen under his breath.

The policeman and the professor

So, in the middle of what was proving to be Inspector Armstrong's most challenging case during his relatively short career as a detective, he found himself lugging a piano that clanked and plinked all the way up the stairs of his lodgings, with two irascible delivery men and an American tourist. "Life's rich tapestry," he thought to himself. Similarly, of all the exciting discoveries and activities Professor Wilson anticipated as part of his trip of a lifetime, this was not one of them.

As the instrument was wheeled into place in his sitting room, Armstrong tipped to the delivery men, apologised again for the inconvenience and then followed them downstairs in order to make his visitor some refreshment.

"So you are a keen musician, Mr. Armstrong," said Wilson as Armstrong re-entered his sitting room with a tray of coffee and biscuits.

"It's Cornelius please," said the policemen.

"Cornelius," repeated the professor with a smile, "and please, call me Woodrow."

Then, answering his guest's original question Armstrong said "I am extremely keen; whether I am competent or not is another matter." He explained the background to his becoming interested in music and the arts, talking openly about his modest upbringing and basic schooling. It was in adulthood therefore where he developed his academic skills as much as possible.

"Yes, I was admiring your collection of books," said Woodrow pointing to the bookcase that stood behind the matching desk at one end of the room. "May I ask what you do for a living Cornelius?"

"I'm a policeman, a detective inspector in fact," said Armstrong trying to sound as humble as he could.

"A detective inspector?" repeated Woodrow, "how impressive and many congratulations. I love it when students take the lead themselves and make the most of their talents. When they exceed them and surprise themselves, it's the most fulfilling part of being a teacher."

"Is that your profession?" asked Cornelius, as he filled the two cups.

"Yes, I'm a professor at Princeton University in New Jersey."

"A professor," exclaimed the policemen, "equally impressive if I may say!"

"I don't think our respective climbing of the career ladders has been so dissimilar," said Woodrow. He explained that he couldn't read until he was twelve, "so perhaps we could both be described as late developers," he said.

"And yet we've clearly done all right for ourselves," added Cornelius. He smiled inwardly at how like-minded people, regardless of backgrounds and nationalities, inevitably gravitate to one another.

His new acquaintance talked about his wife and daughters, and told his host about the busy year it had been for him that had resulted in the slight health scare he had experienced the previous month, which left a slight weakness in his right hand. But through the generosity of his neighbour, Mrs. Brown, the American explained how he had come to be fulfilling this lifetime ambition of visiting the city.

Armstrong replied to his visitor's narrative by sharing with him his own heritage which was a mixture of Border Reiver and – like Wilson – Celtic immigrant. The two agreed that again, they had much in common.

"Dickens appears to be well represented I noticed," said Woodrow, again drawing attention to the bookcase.

"Yes, I must confess my favourite book is Dumas' *The Three Musketeers,* but on the whole, I can't get enough of Dickens's work. I was given a copy of *A Christmas Carol* some years ago as a present, and one thing just led to another."

"I believe he used to begin his novels as periodicals that were printed in episodes over a period of months," said Wilson.

"Yes, so I believe, and as a result it's said that he started a story without ever knowing the end of it; continuously introducing new characters as he went along that ultimately led him to the conclusion. Not unlike police work I suppose."

"Yes dear old Dickens usually found the answers in the end," added the tourist. "One of my favourite writers is your own Mr. Wordsworth," said the tourist, "I intend to visit his cottage if I can get a bicycle sorted out."

"It's beautiful down there in Grasmere," commented Cornelius, "I'm sure Mr. Wheeler will be able to accommodate you when he returns." Then changing the subject, he continued, "So you said you were researching your family history earlier?"

Wilson told him about his grandfather being a preacher in the Congregational Church over seventy years ago, and how his mother was born in the city before the family emigrated in the 1830s. He told his host that he had been trying to find the site of the church and the manse cottage earlier that day but his search had proved unsuccessful.

"I know someone who may be able to help," suggested Cornelius. He explained that by coincidence, Mr. and Mrs. Wheeler actually attended the current Congregational Church on Lowther Street. Furthermore, he said it was the Wheelers who put him in contact with the current minister, the Reverend Wilfred Robinson.

"Reverend Robinson is an accomplished organist," he concluded, "and it is he who is giving me lessons on the piano. He's due to come round and help tune the piano after the service on Sunday but I suppose you'll be planning to have left by then. When you see Mr. Wheeler later I'm sure he can make arrangements for you to see the Reverend, perhaps even before you leave."

Cornelius continued, "I'm a studier of local history myself and I remember the reverend telling me that the site of the old church was just around the corner from here on Annettwell Street" – he indicated the close proximity of the street with a gesture towards the window – "I'm sure he will know more about the history of the church and his predecessors, but we can have a look round there when you've finished your coffee if you like."

"That would be wonderful Cornelius, thank you," said Woodrow, his enthusiasm rekindled by this new lead.

The two walked the short distance to the end of Abbey Street and turned right onto Annettwell Street.

"I'm not sure exactly where the church used to be," said Cornelius, "but it had to be along this strip." He indicated the row of buildings that stretched the few hundred yards between where they were standing and the junction with Castle Street. On the north side of the street were tenement barracks that hid the castle itself from where the two stood at street level. Stopping in front of the Salvation Army barracks halfway along the south side of Annettwell Street, the inspector added, "I think it must have been around here, and presumably the manse cottage would be close by."

Woodrow Wilson stood in silence, taking in the revelation that he was – or was at least extremely near to – the place where his beloved mother had been born. He was surprised how emotional the experience was and as he attempted to speak, he had to subdue a catch in his throat.

"I must confess," he said to his companion, "I do feel an incredible sensation at this moment. My grandfather was the minister here for fifteen years or so – he must have walked along this very street hundreds of times all those years ago."

Amongst their earlier conversation Cornelius had informed Woodrow of the reason for him arriving back at his lodgings in the middle of the afternoon: it was not to take receipt of the piano but to get some rest prior to returning to the station to work through the night. "It's quite an unusual investigation," he had told his visitor, without elaborating further.

Now, he asked the American, "Would you like to return and wait for Mr Wheeler's return."

Wilson looked at the policeman thoughtfully. "You know Cornelius, I think I would like to stay here a while longer by myself if you don't mind. What's more, you need to return and get some rest. Could I beg one more favour? Could you leave a note for Mr. Wheeler to inform him that

I will call again first thing tomorrow morning to organise the hire of the cycle I was telling you about. Perhaps he could also make contact with the Reverend Robinson on my behalf as I would really like to speak with him."

Cornelius agreed and the two arranged to meet again in three weeks' time, when Woodrow's cycling tour of the Lakes was complete and he would return to Carlisle, prior to catching the train back to Glasgow and his sailing home. With a genuinely warm handshake between the two, Cornelius left the visitor to reflect on his discovery.

Suspicions confirmed

Cornelius Armstrong had a natural empathy for his uniformed colleagues; he would constantly ask about their families and their current circumstance, not out of any sense of prurience but out of a genuine interest in their health and wellbeing. This, along with the fact that he had been a bobby himself for five years made him popular with his men, despite the fact that many of them had been in the City Police Force far longer than he had.

It was as though he were destined to achieve a certain status in his career from its commencement eight relatively short years earlier. Not only did Henry Baker see this, but his fellow officers saw it too.

Asked to carry out a sergeant's duties for six months after five years on the beat, and then promoted to detective inspector was unheard of and, although Baker had some difficulty convincing members of the Watch Committee of his decision, everyone within the station seemed to accept it without question. Cornelius had the ability to command respect and tailor his attitude to certain situations while retaining the human touch, instinctively knowing what was required and when. And as his colleagues recognised that he was a cut above the ordinary, there developed an accelerated increase in respect towards him from the men: Armstrong had gone from being "young fella" to "Corny" to "Cornelius" and then to "Inspector" and "Sir" in a matter of a couple of years. It was not something that he had encouraged or sought, but, like Seth Graham and others who knew him and his background, once he was promoted to inspector, Armstrong's colleagues not only voiced their approval, they instantly showed a reverence to his position and a fierce loyalty to him personally, something poor Parker never attained.

PC's Joe Brady and Harry Stokes – who had been instructed by their inspector to re-visit the Stanwix Cemetery, to inspect the site of the first desecration earlier that week – were good examples of this. Both had been in the force longer than Armstrong, but both had the utmost respect for him. Stokes was actually the first constable to whom Armstrong was assigned when he joined the City Force. The two carried out foot patrols during Cornelius's first weeks, and the older man was instantly impressed by the maturity, work ethic and basic common sense demonstrated by his new colleague. Amid the desultory chatter between the two, somewhere between the *where-did-you-grow-ups* and the *do-you-know-so-and-sos*, Cornelius asked Harry if he had any ambition to progress in his role. Stokes explained the dead-men's-shoes system that existed and told him that he was happy with his lot anyway, and he had no particular desire to seek advancement, "Besides," he added, "I don't think I'm clever enough." No sooner had he said the words that old Godfrey Parker popped into his mind – he smiled at the thought which he kept to himself.

As Harry increasingly sensed a kindred spirit between himself and the new man, conversation progressed to family backgrounds: Cornelius shared with his colleague the fact that his father was a soldier with the local regiment who was killed abroad in the mid-seventies. He had originally hoped to follow in his father's footsteps in the military but growing up alone with his mother made him feel obliged to stay in Carlisle in order to look after her. Then, when the "Ripper killings" gripped the country in late 1888, it prompted Cornelius to join the police. A few weeks later, here he was on probation walking the beat with Harry Stokes.

Harry sympathised and shared his own tragedy that saw his wife die giving birth to their son eight years earlier. Stokes had virtually brought the boy up on his own since then, although his mother and sister were a godsend while he was at work. He told Cornelius that, amongst other things, helping the lad with his schooling was a real problem, and it was causing Harry some concern, "I would hate to let his mother down," he said honourably, "she would never forgive me."

Without ever wanting to curry favour with his new colleague, Cornelius offered to help the boy develop his reading. Thereafter, Harry Stokes developed an admiration and appreciation of the skills of the young man, and supported him in his advancement.

Stokes wasn't without influence amongst his colleagues and when they sensed his respect for the new recruit, coupled with their own experiences of his combined altruism and dedication, the respect for the young constable became universal.

Even Joe Brady, who had a well-founded reputation to complain about everything and everyone, would mumble his grudging admiration for Cornelius. Joe's colleagues knew that phrases like "Clever arse!" and "Bloody know-it-all!" constituted high praise from Brady.

As the police wagon crossed Eden Bridges, Brady slapped the reigns on the horse's rump to encourage it up Stanwix Bank; the poor beast managed to haul the heavy wagon and its two passengers with some considerable effort. "Why are we going here again?" asked Brady once they were over the top and heading down Scotland Road toward the cemetery. He had not been party to Armstrong's conversation with Mr. East at Carlisle Cemetery relating to the marked graves.

"The inspector wants us to check if there is any connection between the recent incident and similar ones that took place years ago," replied Stokes.

"How can we do that?"

"Up at the cemetery," Stokes said jerking a thumb over his shoulder, "there was another marked grave beside the one that had been emptied. The old boy up there said it signified that that had been tampered with as well, all those years ago. Cornelius wants us to check if there's any similar up here."

"Sounds a bit cock-eyed to me," harrumphed Brady.

"Everything sounds cock-eyed to you Joe," replied his friend and colleague with a knowing shake of the head.

"Well, I'm just saying…"

"*Well, I'm just saying…*" mimicked Harry rocking his head from side to side.

It was Brady's stock phrase used in most situations: *this tea's not very warm…well I'm just saying; I fetched the logs in yesterday… well I'm just saying; these capes are useless at keeping the water out… well I'm just saying.* It was just something that his colleagues had become used to and amused by over the years, knowing that he meant no harm. Every time he came out with the phrase in the station the other lads on duty would give a cheer, which even amused Brady himself.

He steered the police wagon through the cemetery gates and gave the horse a slap and a rub of thanks as the two climbed down. As with the city's main cemetery, Stanwix was immaculately manicured; except that was for the paupers' area in the far north corner of the site. Like other paupers' plots, with no one to care for it, it had become more than a little neglected and in places, completely overgrown. The grave that had been disturbed earlier in the week contained the remains of one Margaret Bateson. Like Elizabeth Meggs, she was a resident of the workhouse who died in January 1833. The large dark rectangular hole distinguished her burial place from its unkempt neighbours and could easily be seen from across the cemetery. A makeshift cordon had been erected around the plot: it consisted of four metal stakes inserted at each corner of the grave; between each stake drooped a thin rope at waist height. Brady and Stokes approached and stared momentarily into the empty cavern, as if seeking inspiration.

"So what are we looking for again?" asked Brady.

"We need to look at the other graves around this one to see if there is any sign of another disturbance." Stokes described the painted stone he observed at the Carlisle Cemetery and East's description of what it was and what it represented.

The two set about clearing the long tangled grass from the plots adjacent to the Bateson grave. After twenty minutes of barehanded tugging at the dew-soaked greenery, and Harry listening to Joe complaining about "…not having the right tools for a job like this," and asking "...are we supposed to be coppers or gardeners?" Brady found what they were looking for. A few yards away from the open grave, and under a comingled clump of grass, weeds, and moss, was a stone that had been painted red. Although faded after decades of being exposed to the elements, the foliage had afforded it enough protection to retain its reddish hue.

"Isn't that one?" Brady asked his colleague.

Stokes broke off from performing the same task on the other side of the plot to view what Brady had discovered. "Yes, that's exactly it Joe, good lad." The stone and its condition were exactly the same as the one he had seen an hour ago. The two continued to clear the grass and weeds from the new grave. "That should just about do it," announced Stokes after a few minutes. There was now the unusual sight of the empty grave with the cordon round it beside a cleared piece of ground with a faded marker, both of which were surrounded by overgrown plots.

"What now?" asked Brady.

"Let's get cleaned up first," replied Stokes, holding up his wet, dirty hands "there are some rags in the back of the wagon. Then we'll have a look in the chapel to see if we can find anything in there."

After wiping themselves down, Stokes left Brady tending to the horse and went into the church. Referring to the burial register he carefully turned the pages trying not to mark them with his grubby fingers. Each page represented a year; leafing through he stopped at the year in question, 1833. Sure enough there was an asterisk beside the entry directly underneath that of Margaret Bateson. The grave contained one Janet Page. Both she and Bateson were buried on the same day, 25th January 1833.

Which case to investigate?

Cornelius did go to bed in preparation for his nightshift, after leaving Woodrow but, as he anticipated, he didn't get any sleep; the case and the variety of conversation he had enjoyed with his new acquaintance saw to it that the policeman's mind raced for three hours before he gave up the idea around eight o'clock.

He freshened up and went down stairs to find Mr. and Mrs. Wheeler and their young daughter, Emma, relaxing in the parlour after their evening meal.

He apprised Mr. Wheeler of his meeting with the American, the reason for the tourist's visit to Carlisle, and his wish to a hire cycle from Wheeler's shop in order to tour the Lakes. "I suggested he came back in the morning, when you could sort him out with a cycle and perhaps put him in contact with Reverend Robinson," said Cornelius.

"That should be fine," said the shop owner, "I have some touring cycles that should suit him nicely." On the other subject, he continued, "I know the Reverend will be at his church tomorrow so perhaps it would be a good time for him to visit him before he departs."

As her husband was speaking Mrs. Wheeler disappeared for a few moments and returned with a ring containing six large keys. "Your Sergeant Townsend dropped these by earlier Mr. Armstrong," she said as she came back into the room, "he told us you were working tonight. I took the liberty of preparing some sandwiches for you," she added, handing him the keys and a square paper packet.

"Thank you Mrs. Wheeler," said Cornelius. He had developed a close relationship with his host family over the past two years and his housekeeper's kindness never ceased to touch him.

Armstrong spent a further hour chatting to Mr. Wheeler while his wife put their daughter to bed. He then returned to his rooms, donned his outdoor ware and left his lodgings a little before ten o'clock. As well as being a mild night, being mid-summer, there was still a lightness in the sky, which again made him puzzle further over why someone would risk perpetrating a crime like this when there would be a strong possibility of them being observed.

Passing St. Cuthbert's Churchyard he decided to linger a while in a dark doorway on the adjacent Heads Lane where he could see any comings and goings without being seen himself; it was a perfect vantage spot for the purpose of his presence in the quiet corner of the city. After about twenty minutes, with not a soul to be seen, and the inspector believing it was probably too early anyway for such activity, he resolved to return to his hide at regular intervals throughout the night. In the meantime, he decided to carry on to the police station.

The large bunch of keys Townsend had left for his inspector jangled as Armstrong took them out of his pocket upon reaching the front door of the station. It was the only sound that disturbed the eerie quiet on West Walls. He was pleased, but not surprised, that Townsend had left the station clean, neat and tidy; being mainly station-bound the desk sergeant treated the building like a second home.

Despite Townsend's best efforts, the station naturally looked tired having seen better days. The entrance door led to the large main waiting area. To the left were benches lining two walls, predominantly covered with wooden panels that were worn, having had generations of visitors rub against them as they sat waiting to be seen or processed at the large desk that stood opposite the entrance.

Behind the desk was a smaller open area with two or three trestle desks where officers completed any paperwork they had; and some wooden cabinets in which current documentation was held. Previous records were held in a storeroom behind the working area that was accessed via a corridor to the right of the front desk. Chief Constable Henry Baker's office was the last of four rooms that lined the opposite side of the corridor which led to open barred cells at the back of the building. Godfrey Parker's tiny office was immediately beside Baker's, although virtually everyone walked passed the permanently closed door without giving it or its occupant a second thought. Beside Parker's was a room that was used for general meetings, and beside *it*, and almost opposite the front desk, was Armstrong's office.

Cornelius lit a couple of lights in the main area and walked across the creaking timber floor to his office. Like Townsend, Armstrong was fastidious, not only about his appearance but also his modest surroundings; his own office was representative of the whole station but like his sergeant's work area it was neat and tidy.

Laid out on the desk were the papers Townsend had collected on the body snatching cases as per Armstrong's instruction earlier that morning. There were battered old note books, newspapers and loose leafs, all referring to the scandal that had terrified the city some seventy years earlier. Armstrong hoped there may be some clue or lead within them that might guide his current investigation. On top of the pile was an envelope with the Inspector's name on it in Townsend's hand.

Cornelius removed his hat and coat and hung them on the stand behind the door; involuntarily, he gave a shudder and realised, given the lateness of the hour and the emptiness of the building, it wasn't particularly warm after all. In one corner of his office he had small cast iron stove that had an open pipe running up through the ceiling; on top of the stove stood a copper kettle. He brought some logs from a storage area near the cells at the back of the station, lit the stove and lifted the lid of the kettle to check its contents. Satisfied that there was enough water and it was fit for human consumption, he replaced the lid and retrieved his tin mug from his desk drawer.

He glanced through the open doorway of his office at the large clock in the waiting area outside; instinctively he reached for his own fob watch to check it against the clock, it was ten-to-eleven. Armstrong then returned to his desk and sat down to review the information collected by Townsend.

He opened the envelope addressed to him from the desk sergeant that sat on top of the papers. In the note Townsend informed his inspector that PCs O'Hare, Boothman and Kirk were scheduled to be on duty so he had arranged for their colleagues Green, Smith and Watts to guard the cemeteries and graveyards as instructed. He then went to explain what the information in the pile was and where he had sourced it; mainly in what they called the "archive cupboards" in the storeroom, and from records at the public library, as Armstrong had suggested to his sergeant earlier that morning.

The information gathered by Townsend was considerable, given the amount of time that had elapsed since the original body snatching incidents. Armstrong first glanced through the decaying, sepia-coloured newspapers that were so delicate they threatened to come apart in his fingers. Putting them in chronological order he could see how the public's prurience gradually led to fear and revulsion throughout the country.

The earliest reference in the batch of papers came in an article of the *Carlisle Patriot* dated February, 1829. The article covered the hanging of the infamous William Burke a week earlier, and went into great detail about the grisly exploits of him and his accomplice William Hare during the previous two years.

...Despite Burke's continued denials during his trial, it is believed that he and Hare started their criminal career as grave robbers. Whether this is true or not is an academic point, as it has been proved that during the years 1827 and 1828 they murdered up to sixteen people and sold their bodies to medical personnel for dissection. His villainous accomplice Hare escaped prosecution and the gallows by turning King's Evidence.

Armstrong's concentration was broken as the kettle began to whistle. He made himself a mug of coffee and returned to his fascinating study. After reading about Hare's escape his eyebrows were raised when subsequent newspaper articles reported the murderer as residing in Carlisle later in

1829. It was suggested that bereaved relatives took to guarding the body of their family members until it was buried and then they would guard the grave to protect it from violation. The piece concluded that angry mobs were said to have hounded him out of the city by the year's end.

Amid the stories about national atrocities was one local issue that attracted the policeman's attention in an article dated November, 1833. It concerned three incidents of desecration in the city: one each at Stanwix and St. Cuthbert's churchyards and one at Carlisle Cemetery. The guilty parties were two brothers – John Henry Turn and Jacob Turn – who were arrested and tried for the removal of bodies from the three graves. The newspaper took great delight in labelling them "Carlisle's own Resurrection Men," a term coined by the press of the day to describe body snatchers. The story Armstrong read went to great lengths to liken the crimes to that of the notorious Burke and Hare, and the resulting trial to that of William Burke.

The same fate suffered by Burke in 1829 was meted out to eighteen-year-old John Henry Turn four years later in Carlisle. He was tried, found guilty of body snatching and publicly executed at Hangman's Close near the castle. Cornelius suspected that, unlike Burke, young Turn's demise would not have registered outside of his home city. A sentence at the bottom of the article reported that Turn's fourteen-year-old brother Jacob was also found guilty but as he was too young to be hanged, he was deported to Australia instead.

It was now after midnight and Armstrong decided to leave his studying for a while and pay another visit to St. Cuthbert's, after all, if secluded location had demonstrated vulnerability in 1833, why would it be any different for the modern-day grave robbers? He left a light burning in the station, locked the door behind him and walked the short distance to Heads Lane where he retook his secluded lookout.

It proved to be a quiet fifty minutes or so. All in all, two people passed the inspector, neither of whom aware of his presence in the darkened recess. One was a smartly dressed gentleman with white tie and top hat; the intermediate tap of his cane on the flagged surface signalled his purposeful stride before he came into the observer's view. Cornelius couldn't help but wonder where the man had been until such a late hour without a carriage to take him home: *returning home from his club perhaps? Or could it have been an indiscretion that had kept him out?*

Before Cornelius's imagination could go any further, he was disturbed by a shuffling sound approaching his lair. He peeked out discretely and saw a drunk zigzagging his way along the lane; bumping into the churchyard wall on one side, and then stumbling towards the high wall of the building on the other. Fortunately for the policeman – although more through luck than judgement – the drunk's erratic ambulatory pattern took him away from the doorway at the key moment and therefore didn't compromise the observer's hiding position.

Content that the surrounding environs were clear Cornelius appeared from his hiding place and walked quietly up the lane, onto Blackfriars Street and then entered the churchyard itself. The dim gaslights, combined with the light summer night gave the inspector sufficient visual capacity to survey the area; there was no sign of any wrongdoing anywhere inside or outside the churchyard. It was the first of four such inspections he carried out at various points throughout the night, all with the same negative outcome. Neither disappointed, nor contented, Inspector Armstrong returned to the station after each surveillance.

On one occasion, around three o'clock, he returned to find a note on his desk from PC Danny O'Hare informing his superior that he had locked a burglar up in the cells. It was common for the constables carrying out a night beat to have keys for the station for this very purpose. O'Hare had locked the man up and returned to his duties by the time the inspector let himself back in. Armstrong checked on the villain who was already laid out, dozing, and returned to his office to resume his reading.

His original thinking in asking Townsend to gather the information was to see if any patterns or clues could be obtained; but now Armstrong found he was fascinated in the histories in their own right, regardless of current circumstances. Some of the papers related to the passing of the Anatomy Act in 1832. One report in particular explained that the Act was in direct response to the scale of the body snatchers' work; one gang in London admitted to stealing between five hundred and a thousand bodies over a twelve year period. It was stated that up to ten guineas was received for each cadaver. The Act thus allowed for bodies to be donated to medical science, negating the need for the illegal activity.

The date of the Act prompted Armstrong to sift through the papers looking for the Turn case he read about earlier. One of the loose leaves in the bundle was a tattered sheet that appeared to be a written confession by John Henry Turn; the handwriting was neat and confident but at the bottom of the page it was marked with a simple X.

Armstrong noted that although Turn and his brother were found guilty of body snatching, it was never established to whom they sold the bodies. *What did they do with them? What's more, why would they be raiding tombs at all when the Anatomy Act was passed the previous year?*

Information shared

Following a stunning sunrise earlier, the sun shone in a beautiful azure sky as Sergeant Bill Townsend arrived at the station at seven o'clock. More often than not he was the first officer there; his night-beat constables usually ambled in about half an hour later. On this morning however he walked in to the sound of chatter and laughter.

Inspector Armstrong was in his office while to the rear of the front desk, PCs Green, Smith and Watts were sharing with each other their experiences from the previous night over a brew. Once Sergeant Townsend had sorted his papers out for the day ahead and poured himself a cup of tea, Armstrong called the group into the meeting room, conscious that he had agreed to brief the Chief Constable upon his arrival.

"First, Bill," he said turning to Townsend, once the men were all seated, "thanks for the papers you sorted out for me yesterday. I'm not sure if they help us with our current predicament but they certainly made for interesting reading."

"No problem sir," replied Townsend, "as you suggested there were a few bits and bobs in the archive cupboards but the main bulk of the information came from the library." As an afterthought, he added, "Oh that reminds me, old Sydney Irvine asked me to send his regards and hoped that you enjoyed the present from your relation."

Cornelius looked blankly towards Townsend and gave a confused gesture that was a combination of a sharp headshake and shoulder-shrug, which prompted Townsend to elaborate.

"He said something about a relative of yours who was in the library a couple of weeks ago asking about you."

As Armstrong had very few relatives, this extra comment did nothing to clarify the situation, "I don't know what he's talking about," he said with another shake of the head. He decided, if he remembered that is, to call into the library on his way back to his lodgings and clear up the confusion by speaking with Sydney in person.

In the meantime he turned to the matter of the previous evening, thanked the constables for their sense of duty at such short notice, and asked each of them to report their observations. It transpired that there wasn't a great deal to report.

Bobby Green had been despatched to Upperby Cemetery in the south of the city. He didn't admit to his superior officer that at one point he had fallen asleep on a bench beside St John's Church but instead chose to risk the obvious quiet-as-the-grave crack: Armstrong and his colleagues looked at Green nonplussed at his stupidity.

William Smith had a similarly non-eventful night at the cemetery on Dalston Road. Having been raided just a few days before, Armstrong felt it unlikely the robbers would strike there again, but the large sixty- acre site provided plenty of opportunity for the latter day resurrectionists, should they choose to strike again. As it was, the only noteworthy observation was a family of foxes Smith saw roaming at the furthest point of the cemetery. Again, Armstrong trained his piercing blue eyes on the constable. No words were required.

The only bit of policing that was actually done during the night had been performed by Sam Watts who was watching over the Stanwix Cemetery.

"It was around half past two; I was round the back of the church..." the familiar look from his superior officer told Watts he was about to give too much information. "Anyway I heard a shuffle and grunting sound coming from the far wall of the churchyard. I er...finished doing what I was doing and came back around the side. I squinted in the darkness and could just make out a dark figure scrambling over the wall.

"Naturally I thought this was it: *I've got him.* But no sooner had the thought crossed my mind when I saw another figure clamber over the wall after him. I suddenly realised it was Danny O'Hare giving chase to the bloke. I came out of my hiding space and the bloke saw me and changed direction; Danny calls over to me to grab him and I managed to head him off and rugby-tackle him to the ground." Then, looking down at his muddied trousers wistfully he added, "I don't think the missus is going to be too impressed mind you." He continued his narrative.

"It turns out Danny had disturbed the bloke attempting a burglary in one of those villas on Scotland Road; he tore off when he saw O'Hare and tried to take a short cut to wherever he was going through the churchyard."

Armstrong blew out his cheeks in frustration at a mainly fruitless evening's work. Having had that initial disappointing thought flash through his mind, and knowing that Godfrey Parker had been – as he put it – "looking into" a series of break-ins in the area over the past few months, he at least consoled himself with the fact that they may have apprehended the perpetrator; not that dear old Godfrey had anything to do with it of course.

"Well, thanks lads," he said at last, "I appreciate your efforts. I'll let Inspector Parker know that we've probably got his man and he can follow it up later when he gets in," – a comment that prompted a few darting eyes and half smiles between the uniforms – "in the meantime, you blokes go home and get some rest; and thanks again." Almost as an afterthought, he said to Sergeant Townsend, "Bill, I think it would be best to keep up the night patrols for the next few nights. If something happens and we haven't made reasonable efforts to prevent it, we'll get heavily criticised."

"Very good, sir," replied Townsend, "I'll sort it out and let all the lads know."

To the sound of the dull rubbing noise of the chairs against the worn floorboards, the uniformed officers left their Inspector to ponder the latest position. The fact was that he didn't have any more information now than he had yesterday when he spoke with the Chief Constable. After a few minutes he rose and went next door into his own office. As he did so, by chance, Godfrey Parker entered the station.

"Ah Godfrey," said Armstrong, "I had some extra lads on last night to try to catch the body snatchers. We had no luck but I think we may have stumbled across your burglar."

Parker removed his hat as his colleague addressed him – an involuntary gesture of inadequacy that embarrassed both men. His action revealed a high forehead under which was a kindly yet dateless face. He smiled at Cornelius who felt he was not only unaware of the grave robbing, he had probably forgotten about the burglaries. He felt compelled to explain further.

"There's been a series of break-ins north of the river; you told me you were looking into them?"

"Oh yes, Cornelius I remember now," said the older man.

"Well I think we've got your man. He's in the cells at the back," he gestured with a thumb over his shoulder, "maybe you could question him later?" Armstrong knew that if it were anyone else informing Parker of the villain in the cell, they would no doubt mischievously advise him to be careful when entering. He refrained from making the comment Parker must have heard hundreds of times during his career.

"Oh yes, that's a good idea Cornelius, I'll do that," said his colleague, "thank you very much for your help."

The two Inspectors retreated to their respective offices, lost in their own respective thoughts. Their Chief Constable arrived at the station around nine o'clock and summoned Armstrong to his office as he walked down the corridor.

"I need an update Cornelius," said the large man levering himself out of is overcoat, "I am meeting with the Chairman of the Watch Committee in an hour and then with the editors from the *Journal* and the *Patriot* later this morning at the Town Hall.

"There's not a great deal to report I'm afraid, sir," said the inspector. Although he was comfortably on first name terms with his superior officer, both men knew that when official titles were used it was usually bad news. Armstrong updated Baker about his visit to the carter's yard the previous morning and the possible line of enquiry that produced. Then there was the previous night's activity with the apparent breakthrough with the series of burglaries but nothing regarding progress with the bigger case. "I've asked Townsend to arrange for extra guard patrols to continue for the next few nights," he added.

"I suppose there's not much more we can do at this stage," said Baker resignedly, sitting down at his desk. He thought for a while before musing out loud, "I'm surprised the newspapers haven't made more of the story yet, but that won't continue I'm sure; if there is another event I think they'll start stoking the public up. That's all we'll need, vigilantes roaming the streets after dark."

Cornelius recalled the fifty or so people who had gathered round the gravesite at Carlisle Cemetery the previous morning and concurred with his superior's view. Rather than articulate it however, he simply gave an audible nod. "If that'll be all sir, I'll get myself and home and get some rest." With an agreement to meet with the Chief Constable at the same time tomorrow – assuming there were no further developments in the meantime – Armstrong took his leave of Baker.

He returned to his office and couldn't resist glances through some of the information again. Seeing that he was sitting at his desk through his open door, PC Harry Stokes approached his office. The inspector was sitting at his desk deep in thought, tweaking the horns of his moustache.

"'Scuse me sir, I never got the chance to speak with you yesterday after Joe and me went up to Stanwix."

"Ah, Harry, how did you come on?" said Armstrong looking up.

"Sure enough," said Stokes, "the grave that was disturbed the other night was beside another one that had a red stone." He referred to his notebook, "It contained the remains of one Janet Page; it had been dug up…"

"In 1833," interrupted Armstrong.

"That's right, sir," said Stokes, "How did you know that?"

Cornelius gestured towards the papers on his desk "Harry, I'm not sure if I'm investigating a crime from the 1890s or one from the 1830s."

A distinctive figure

Sydney Irvine had worked in the city library at Tullie House all of his working life. A natural academic, he attended the grammar school as a boy and had the opportunity been there, would probably have graced one of the country's top universities. But it wasn't to be and as it turned out, a quieter life and a long career in the library of his home city awaited Sydney. Not that he minded; his wealth of knowledge combined with a natural humility made him a popular figure with colleagues and the public alike. As the end of the century approached, then so did his sixtieth year and a service of over forty years had seen him progress to a position of senior librarian.

Sydney had a snowy thatch of hair that was raked over to cover his balding crown. From the end of his nose were permanently perched a small *pince-nez* and he wore a baggy old cardigan that his colleagues joked was a present when he first started as a junior all those years ago.

The first job he helped with every morning was to replace the books that had been returned the previous day to their appropriate shelves. He was re-arranging some in the local history section and was about to step onto a wheeled-ladder that was used to reach the higher shelves when he heard the voice behind him, "Good morning, Sydney."

He turned to find a familiar face smiling at him, "Mr. Armstrong, good morning to you, I haven't seen you in a while."

Cornelius had become good friends with the librarian over the years. After his modest childhood schooling he set about educating himself in adulthood. A natural magnet for this desire to learn was the library and for well over a decade he had been a frequent visitor, picking Sydney's brains on subjects as diverse as the sciences and local history, to the classics and natural history. This approach to learning had allowed Cornelius to identify his favourite subjects which in turn, had led him to start his own collection of books; a collection which now filled a bookcase along one wall of his sitting room

That morning, as he was putting the key in the front door of his lodgings after returning from his night shift, the policeman suddenly remembered Bill Townsend's cryptic comment about Sydney's message concerning a relative of Armstrong. As the rear gardens of Tullie House, backed on Abbey Street, Cornelius decided to pay the librarian a visit to ask about the encounter. He replaced his keys in his pocket, crossed the street and walked through the tall wrought iron gates that led into the gardens and through an arch towards the main entrance.

Responding to Sydney's greeting Cornelius explained, "No, I've been particularly busy for the past few weeks." He got straight down to the purpose of his calling. "My sergeant, Bill Townsend, was in yesterday on my behalf."

"Yes," said the librarian, "I gave him some information about the body snatchers of the 1830s. I assumed it is to do with these recent incidents?"

"Yes, I'm afraid it is. They're proving to be a bit of a puzzle I must admit. However, that's not really what I want to know about. Townsend said that you had passed a message on about a relative of mine?"

"Oh yes, that's right," recalled Sydney, "he was in here…oh, let me think," he put his forefinger to his lips and leant on a rung of the ladder, deep in thought. "It must have been about a fortnight ago. He came in and asked about you; said he was a distant cousin who you hadn't seen for a long time and, knowing it was your birthday soon, he wanted to surprise you with a present. He wasn't sure what your tastes were however so he wanted some guidance on what might be appropriate."

As an afterthought Sydney asked, "Did you see him?"

"No," said Cornelius, completely bemused by the story. "It obviously wasn't George?" he asked referring to his cousin, who was a sergeant in the Border Regiment and who was known to Sydney Irving.

"No, it certainly wasn't Sergeant Armstrong," confirmed the librarian.

"Did he give a name?" asked the policeman – then in response to his friend's downturned mouth and shake of the head – "what did he look like?"

Again Sydney thought for a while. "I remember he was quite a distinctive chap actually. Even before he approached me I became aware of his presence; he wouldn't blend into a crowd, put it that way," he said with a half-smile. He continued his recollection.

"He was a well-built fellow, I would say about your age. He wore a long Inverness Cape and a flat topped hat with a wide brim. His hair was quite long and I remember he had a sort of stubble on his face that was perfectly manicured. It was nowhere near like a full beard, more like an immaculately trimmed shadow. As I say…quite distinctive.

I never gave much thought to the matter until your sergeant called in yesterday."

Cornelius thanked the librarian and promised he would meet him for a cup of coffee sometime within the next few weeks, when things had quietened down a little.

As he was crossing Abbey Street back to his lodgings Mr. Wheeler came out of his cycle shop immediately next door. "Good morning Cornelius, did you have a good night?"

"Morning, Jack," the policeman wore a weary smile, "I'm not sure to be honest. It was interesting without being terribly productive. We did have one success but too many questions have been thrown up and I'm afraid answers appear to be in short supply. More of a good history lesson if anything," he said cryptically, which rather lost Jack Wheeler. Instead, he changed the subject.

"Your Mr. Wilson called by earlier. I fixed him up with a cycle for his tour round the Lakes; said he would be back in three weeks. A real nice chap he was. I also made contact with Reverend Robinson on his behalf and the American gentleman said he would call round to see him this morning before he set off for Penrith…said something about meeting some people there."

It was now mid-morning and Cornelius was starting to wonder if he was ever going to get to bed. "That's good," he said politely, "I'm glad things are working out for him. We did arrange to meet upon his return so no doubt I'll catch up with him then." Now if you'll excuse me Jack, I think I'll turn in."

"Yes, no problem lad, you go and get some kip," replied the shop owner cheerfully.

No sooner had Cornelius climbed the few steps and entered his lodgings, he was met by Mrs. Wheeler who was equally enthusiastic to see her lodger as her husband had been a few moments earlier.

"Mr. Armstrong!" she exclaimed, "I thought you'd be home hours ago…I assumed you were in bed so haven't been up to your rooms."

"No, it proved quite a long night Mrs. Wheeler; I'm just about to turn in now."

"Let me make you a nice cup of tea before you do," she said, "I'm just about to take our Jack one next door."

Without the energy to protest, Cornelius acquiesced and thanked his housekeeper again for the sandwiches she had made up for him the night before. He waited in the kitchen while his housekeeper made the tea and then took a mug upstairs. Easing himself out of his outdoor ware, he slumped into his rocking chair by the unlit fire and – despite his frustrations with the case – smiled with contentment.

He was pleased he had called on Sydney; and passed the time of day with Mr. and Mrs. Wheeler; and he was happy that his new acquaintance Woodrow Wilson was having a productive holiday. Although he enjoyed his own company, he liked being acquainted with good, decent people. Even the lads at the station made it worthwhile. They all inspired him in their own way.

He finally climbed into bed with the intention of sleeping for a few hours and then going back into the station during the late afternoon to check on any developments and ensure plans were in place for the cemetery guarding later that night.

Discomfort and confusion

Herbert Underwood was a magistrate of long standing in the city; he was also Chairman of the Watch Committee. As well as Underwood, the committee was made up of half a dozen crusty old councillors – all of whom had deputies of course – and a solicitor and fellow magistrate, George Sowerby. Together, their role was to oversee the activity of the city police force.

Henry Baker himself was well-known to the committee, given his length of service and solid track record. They were delighted with his appointment to the post of chief constable two years earlier and settled back into their comfortable chairs with brandy and cigars, believing that the status quo enjoyed for the previous two decades under Baker's predecessor would be maintained. They soon found themselves fidgeting uncomfortably however, when one of Baker's first decisions was to appoint a thirty-year-old temporary sergeant to the role of his replacement as detective inspector

Ever since the new man's decision, the committee had kept a close eye on Baker, and a closer one still on Armstrong. Cornelius was not the clubbable type; not someone who would simply fall into line as and when he was required to do so by his elders and betters. Instead he was comfortable in his own skin and his vocational attitude to his duties regularly resulted in him doing what he believed was the right thing; not the easy thing or the popular thing, but the right thing. All of which led to some in authority viewing the young policeman with an element of circumspection. Not that the young detective had put a foot wrong in the time he had been in the senior post, but that did nothing to assuage the suspicions of the traditionalists regarding change and innovation: it might work in other places but it wasn't for Carlisle.

It was something that Baker and Armstrong had discussed at length at the time of the appointment and the two were prepared for the close scrutiny – and so it was to prove. Every time Baker attended his informal meetings with Herbert Underwood, the chairman would continually ask about Armstrong; and whenever there was a formal meeting of the Watch Committee and the chief constable was required to give an update on policing in the city, Armstrong's work was scrutinised to the nth degree. It inwardly amused Henry Baker that in all the meetings he had attended, he had never once been asked about Detective Inspector Godfrey Parker's work. The injustice of this, regarding Armstrong's performance, was offset by a certain amount of relief as far as Baker was concerned; for if such a question were ever put to him, he would never be quite sure how to answer it.

As far as Armstrong was concerned, he appreciated the support and protection he received from his friend and mentor Henry Baker, and concentrated on doing his job, rather than worry about what the committee thought of him. Their suspicion of the young detective was reciprocated by Armstrong who believed most of them were more interested in having a street or a bridge in the city named after them than serving the citizens to any great extent.

It was against this uncomfortable background that Henry Baker prepared to meet Herbert Underwood on this particular morning during the summer of 1896. The disturbance of the first grave at Stanwix earlier in the week had attracted the attention of Underwood and his colleagues after it had been reported in the local newspapers. Then, once the second such incident occurred in the city's main cemetery, the chairman had no hesitation in summoning the Chief Constable to ask what was being done about it.

It was shaping up to be the most significant crime to date as far as Baker's tenure was concerned, and more importantly, the most serious in Cornelius Armstrong's short investigative career. Baker knew he was in for a difficult meeting, and so it would prove.

"So who is carrying out this investigation Henry?" asked Underwood, once he and the chief constable had exchanged the briefest of pleasantries. Both of them knew it was a choreographed game: a process they were going through to get to an answer both were fully aware of. Baker also knew by drawing out the process, the chairman was taking the full opportunity to question the capabilities of Baker's young subordinate.

"Detective Inspector Armstrong," he replied firmly, giving Armstrong his full title, as if to emphasise his confidence in him; it was more game playing but necessary in the circumstance. If Baker were a betting man he would have also collected on Underwood's next question.

"Do you think he's up to it? After all he's very inexperienced. The city hasn't seen anything like this for generations and it could cause panic if it is not nipped in the bud. The Watch Committee…"

"Armstrong is a good policeman," interrupted the Chief Constable, without apology, unwilling as he was to listen to more pontificating by the committee and their reservations. He had to refrain from asking if they would prefer Godfrey Parker to investigate the matter but rather than antagonise Underwood simply added, "I have every confidence that he can solve the matter as quickly as possible."

It was a bold statement from Baker as he was aware that there were no firm lines of enquiry yet. However, he went through the work so far, including the extra night patrols and to his pleasant surprise, the chairman appeared to understand and accept the approach that was being taken.

Once the two had finished their meeting, they were scheduled to meet with the editors of the two local newspapers to brief them on this and other issues. As they were awaiting the arrival of their visitors Underwood couldn't resist offering his usual veiled threat, "I just hope this is resolved quickly, Henry, for both your sakes."

Baker noted Underwood's use of the word *your*, as opposed to the word *our*.

*

Cornelius was awakened by a light knocking on his door. "Mr. Armstrong? Mr. Armstrong, sir, you have a visitor."

Cornelius recognised the voice of his housekeeper and groggily looked at the clock: it was just after half past two. Although he had only been in bed for less than four hours he had enjoyed a deep sleep and, despite originally intending to get up around four o'clock, felt refreshed enough to begin an afternoon's work.

"Just a minute, Mrs. Wheeler," he called getting out of bed and reaching for his dressing gown.

Opening his sitting room door, his housekeeper was standing on the first floor landing, looking a little embarrassed at having woken her lodger. "I'm sorry to bother you sir, but you have a visitor. Reverend Robinson has popped round to tune your new piano."

The seemingly random words took their time to register with the policeman, such was his bleary state. Mrs. Wheeler paused in order for him to comprehend what she was saying. Gradually, he remembered that the minister had offered to help him tune the piano he had had delivered the previous afternoon. The realisation triggered thoughts of the American, Professor Wilson; the ridiculous situation of them carrying the instrument up to his rooms; Wilson's search for his family history, and the fact that his grandfather was one of Reverend Robinson's predecessors.

He then wanted to ask why the minister was here today when he had arranged to come on Saturday afternoon but realised it was a question Mrs. Wheeler could neither answer, nor would be interested in. Instead, he accepted the situation with a scratch of the head and rub of the forehead. "Thank you Mrs. Wheeler, would you mind making the Reverend a cup of tea while I get dressed?"

"Certainly Mr. Armstrong, I'll give you fifteen minutes before sending him up," said the housekeeper heading towards the stairs.

The Reverend Wilfred Robinson was the archetypal doddering old clergyman; he walked with a permanent stoop, and had unruly white whiskers that horseshoed around his large ears, which he would instinctively cock towards anyone who was conversing with him. A source of much amusement to his congregation and music pupils however was his change in character once he was sitting in front of a piano or organ: a natural musician, he would sway and dip on his stool as he lived the piece he was playing.

Cornelius had been receiving piano lessons from Reverend Robinson for six months after he had been introduced to him by Jack and Isabella Wheeler who attended the Congregational Church on Lowther Street. The two got on well, Cornelius was making good progress, and when he told the Reverend that he was investing in his own instrument, Robinson shared his enthusiasm by offering to help tune it once it was in place, and hold lessons at Cornelius's lodgings thereafter. This was all very much appreciated by Cornelius – it's just that he could have done without the Reverend calling on this particular day.

"Good afternoon, Cornelius," said Reverend Robinson, after he had climbed the stairs following his discrete cup of tea, "I hope you don't mind me calling, unheralded, as it were. I know we originally arranged it for Saturday but I couldn't wait to see the new *Broadwood*. It's not too inconvenient is it?"

"No, not at all Wilfred," lied Armstrong, "please come in."

Robinson was suitably impressed with the beautiful piano and was in his element as he tweaked, tapped and listened to each note, all the while making desultory conversation with his host.

Due to a combination of sleep deprivation and his mind being on other matters, Cornelius was paying only slight attention to some of the things his guest was saying. That was until the clergyman said something that caused the policeman to snap out of his torpor.

"I met that young Professor Wilson this morning," he said, "the American chap. He had been sent round to me by Jack; looking into his family history he was."

"Yes," said Armstrong, "I was talking to him yesterday; seems a nice fellow."

"Indeed," agreed Robinson. "I didn't know which one he was at first. I was pottering about in the sacristy when the verger came in and told me there was someone to see me. When I went out into the church, there were two men standing talking to one another at the entrance. As it turned out, Mr. Wilson had just met the other man by chance who shook his hand warmly as I approached and left without introducing himself to me." The Reverend paused and added, almost to himself, "Quite a distinctive fellow he was."

It was this last comment that captured Cornelius's attention, after only paying slight attention to Wilfred's rambling recollections. "*Distinctive?*" he repeated, being reminded of Sydney Irving's description of the visitor to the library some weeks earlier, "In what way?"

"*Uh?*" mumbled Robinson, stirred from his own day-dreaming, "Oh, he had unusual collar-length hair and wore a long Inverness cape. When Mr. Wilson introduced himself to me, I asked if his friend would be joining us. He explained that the meeting was by chance; then he said something quite strange. He explained that the man – who didn't give a name incidentally – was originally vising the church also to speak to me.

"However, as I approached the two, he didn't wait to introduce himself, instead made an excuse to Mr. Wilson and left. The American chap then said something further that neither of us understood. During their ten-minute encounter at the church door, and once Mr Wilson had explained the purpose of his visit and his experiences in Carlisle so far, the stranger spent virtually the whole time asking him questions about you, Cornelius."

The Workhouse

A new day saw Cornelius walking through Caldewgate towards St. Mary's Workhouse, following another lead in the body snatching case. It had developed the previous afternoon, following the time spent with Reverend Robinson at his lodgings.

Around four o'clock he returned to the station to check on any developments and see how Henry Baker's meeting had gone that morning. Upon his arrival, he knew immediately as the chief constable said, "Ah, Detective Inspector, come in and close the door." Armstrong knew when Henry was serious about an issue, as he had a habit of letting him know by addressing him with his formal title. It was a little game he played, partly tongue-in-cheek, partly reminding his subordinate of their respective positions. Cornelius always understood the need for the performance and invariably replied in kind.

"How did it go this morning, sir?" he asked, sitting down opposite Baker.

"It was as uncomfortable as expected I'm afraid," replied Henry. He proceeded to tell Armstrong about the meeting with Underwood; about the continuous doubting of Armstrong's abilities, and the unsubtly veiled threats. He then covered the subsequent meeting with the editors of the *Journal* and the *Patriot*, which had proved a little more successful.

Although reporters for the newspapers were happy to follow the lead of the Watch Committee and continually have the odd dig at the young inspector, Baker had developed a good understanding with their superiors and this working relationship allowed him to request moderation in some of the column inches. In this case he was keen to avoid panic amongst the readership that may well lead to vigilante groups forming as it had earlier in the century. The newspaper men understood the issue and agreed to Baker's request on the understanding that they too were kept fully informed of any developments.

"So all in all, we have bought ourselves a little bit of time, Cornelius, but I need this sorted out quickly," concluded the chief constable, rising from his desk which signified the end of his working day.

"Understood sir," said Armstrong.

Cornelius walked back along the corridor to his own office to find a good quality white envelope addressed to him lying on his desk. Taking the paper knife from the top draw he slit it open. Inside was a brief note, in an educated hand, inviting him to inspect the records of the St Mary's Workhouse, claiming that it would help in resolving the case of the "grave disturbers." The note was signed "JC".

Armstrong instinctively reached into his waistcoat pocket for his watch: it was now after five and probably too late to follow the matter up. He went to the open door of his office and called, "Bill, who delivered this?" He waved the note at his desk sergeant.

"I don't know, sir," replied Bill Townsend, "I'd popped out the back around two o'clock and by the time I returned, it was sitting here on the front desk. No explanation, no nothing."

The Inspector slumped back down at his desk and again glanced through the papers on his desk, absentmindedly reaching for the horns of his moustache as he did so – always a sign of deep concentration. He had no alternative but to leave this latest annoyingly vague line of enquiry until the morning.

*

The austere St Mary's Workhouse was built over a century earlier to house the workers who had fallen below the poverty line. Within thirty years of its establishment, it was burgeoning with handloom weavers who had been forced out of employment through the advance of technology, and veteran soldiers returning from the Napoleonic Wars. The only thing that had changed in the seventy or so intervening years was its condition. It was crumbled and rotten in places yet retained its imposing presence in the impoverished Irish quarter of the city.

The large, double doors housed a smaller single access point. The gatekeeper responded to Armstrong's banging and the policeman stepped over the large timber lip. Explaining the purpose of his visit, he was escorted across the cobbled courtyard to the office of the warden, Peter Fletcher, a middle-aged man with an eager expression and a welcoming manner.

"Ah, good morning, Inspector," he said as they were introduced by the gatekeeper. He rose from his desk, offered a hand, gestured toward a chair opposite and then reached up to a shelf to retrieve a large leather-bound ledger. "I was told that you might pay us a call; I have the records to hand," he said sitting back down and placing the ledger on the battered wooden desk between then.

Armstrong was naturally surprised by the comment, "By whom?" he asked.

"A gentleman came here a few days ago, asking to look at these records. He said you might be following him."

"Did he say why he wanted to see them?"

"He claimed he was doing some family research. Before he left, he said I might be receiving a visit from the police but didn't explain why. He was gone before I had a chance to ask him."

"Where was he from?" asked the inspector.

"He didn't say, but he didn't sound local."

"Can I see the records he looked at please?"

"Yes, of course, these are the ones right here." Fletcher opened the ledger on a page he had already marked with a ruler and swung the book round so Cornelius could read it. The warden then indicated the page that was in front of the policeman headed "1833." He added, "The man didn't say very much, or even who he was looking for, but once he studied this document, he seemed satisfied that his investigations were over."

Armstrong studied the page from the top. It was a list of "residents" from the year in question. The sixth name on the list was the first that he recognised: Lizzie Meggs. The page was split into four columns, listing the name, condition, age and whereabouts of the individual. Beside Lizzie's name was simply written the word "Deceased"; her age was given as 25 and it was stated that she was buried in Carlisle Cemetery. Armstrong instinctively reached for his pocket book and turned to the page on which he took some notes at the cemetery. Mr. East had told him that the grave beside Elizabeth Meggs that had been disturbed in 1833 was that of Elsie Grimes; looking back at the leger the next entry under that of the unfortunate Meggs was that of the equally unfortunate Grimes.

Flicking forward a couple of pages in his notebook the Inspector reminded himself that it was Margaret Bateson's grave that had been disturbed in Stanwix earlier that week. The grave beside it inspected by his Constables Brady and Stokes once contained the remains of a Janet Page. Cross-referencing the names with those in the ledger they inevitably matched. As with Lizzie Meggs, the single word of explanation and their respective ages were listed against their names; the only difference being their whereabouts was given listed as Stanwix Cemetery. Underneath the entry of Janet Page were two more females, Lilly Carrick and Cissy Henderson. They were also listed as deceased with their resting place indicated as St. Cuthbert's Churchyard.

Armstrong jotted their names down as a matter of course and noted that all of the women were under thirty at the time of their passing. He leant on one arm of his chair, and tweaked one of the horns of his moustache, while staring into the middle distance.

"Is it of any interest Mr. Armstrong?" Peter Fletcher broke the slightly embarrassing silence.

"Sorry," said Cornelius snapping out of his reverie, "I think so, yes," although inwardly the detective wasn't really sure. "Tell me," he said slightly changing the subject, "what did this other man look like?" He had a feeling he knew the answer already but asked the question, regardless.

"He was a well-dressed man, I would say in his thirties," replied Fletcher. "I remember he wore his hair slightly longer than normal and had a very thin beard."

"Quite distinctive, you might say," added Armstrong with a frustrated air.

"Yes, I think that's the word actually – distinctive," agreed the Warden, obviously not being party to Armstrong's previous conversations regarding the stranger.

"Thank you for your time Mr. Fletcher, it's been very helpful," said Cornelius turning the ledger back round, signifying their meeting was over.

"You're welcome sir," said the Warden, a little bemused by the whole thing.

The two shook hands and the Inspector turned to leave; then as an afterthought he asked, "I don't suppose the man left a name?"

"Yes he did actually," replied Fletcher much to Armstrong's surprise. The warden opened the top drawer of the desk and shuffled through some papers until he found the scrap that he was looking for, "Here it is," he said holding it up, "I remember because it was quite distinctive too. It was John Chivery."

Armstrong was taken aback for a moment in surprised amusement. "John Chivery?" he repeated. "That's a character from a Dickens novel." The avid reader was referring to the turnkey of the Marshalsea Prison in *Little Dorrit*. It was obviously something Fletcher was unaware of but Armstrong suddenly recognised the game the stranger was playing, choosing a name that was in keeping with the surroundings of the workhouse.

He thanked Peter Fletcher again and took his leave. On his way back to the station he decided to detour through neighbouring Shaddongate and visit Seth Graham again to double check some information the carter had given him during his previous visit. After the usual pleasantries and Armstrong's polite refusal of a mug of tea, he asked Seth for a description of the man who paid for the hire of a cart that was never used.

"Could've done with a haircut if you ask me," replied Seth.

Armstrong smiled to himself at the thought of Seth Graham passing an opinion on someone else's appearance. The policeman then flicked back through the pages of his notebook, "And his name, Seth, you said it was..." then finding the page, "...Gridley."

"Yes that's right," recalled the carter, "that's what he said, Mr. Gridley."

Inspector Armstrong left the carter's yard with a strange feeling that he was somehow making progress in his investigation.

Cause for optimism

"I believe we do have a suspect, sir." Cornelius Armstrong was back in his chief constable's office briefing his superior on the latest developments. He informed Henry Baker of the four independent witnesses who had all provided a virtually identical description of the same man.

"Initially, it looked as though this man was bizarrely interested in me personally," continued the inspector, citing his encounter with Sydney Irving at the library, "I can't explain that, but once I'd visited old Seth Graham's place and the workhouse, it's clear there is a connection between him and the case. He actually paid for a hiring from Seth – although he never actually used the cart. He then spoke to Fletcher about residents of the workhouse in the 1830s, and the page that he had been scrutinising contained the names of Lizzie Meggs, Maggie Bates, Elsie Grimes and Janet Page – all young women whose graves were either desecrated in 1833 or earlier this week."

Baker looked reassuringly intrigued by Armstrong's narrative. He asked the obvious question, "Do we have a name?"

Armstrong took in a deep breath, knowing that his convincing theory could now be unpicked, "This is where it gets a little strange," he said cautiously, "he has given two aliases so far; both of them appear to be characters from Dickensian books."

"*What?*"

"One was a character who worked at a prison in *Little Dorrit*," explained Cornelius, "not surprisingly he gave that as his name to the warden at the workhouse. The other name he gave to Seth was Gridley – he was an obscure character in *Bleak House*. I'm not sure if you've read it sir, but the character is constantly complaining that his case won't be heard. It's a bit tenuous but I wonder if this stranger is trying to tell us something."

"No, I'm not a Dickens' man myself," said the Chief Constable irritably, "it all sounds a bit fanciful to me Cornelius. Are you sure you know where you are going with this?"

"It's probably the best line we have sir; a suspect who not only makes no attempt to disguise his appearance and seems to make himself known wherever he goes. Then there are these seemingly ridiculous clues he leaves behind. Ridiculous maybe but as we have nothing else to follow at this stage, I would like to explore it a little further."

Baker's faith and trust in his inspector was being tested but knowing that Cornelius was right in saying there was nothing else to go on, he instructed Armstrong to carry on as he saw fit. "But keep me informed at every stage, Detective Inspector," he said dismissing his man.

There it was again: the formal title that left Cornelius in no doubt about the height of the stakes and the consequences of making a mess of the investigation. He returned to his office to reflect on the information.

Back at his desk, Inspector Armstrong went through all of the information available to him once more. One thing that Baker had taught him during his early days as a detective was to continually go back to the start of the case and retain it as the fixed point. "Otherwise, you go off on tangents that eventually become wild goose chases and you forget what you were supposed to be doing in the first place," Henry had told him.

With this in mind, Cornelius decided to go back up to Stanwix Cemetery, where the first grave was disturbed. He grabbed his hat and coat and called to Sergeant Townsend, "Bill, I'm going back up to Stanwix Cemetery." Before Townsend had a chance to respond, he was gone.

The inspector set off walking with the intention of catching a tram along the way. As none was forthcoming an hour's walk found him standing at the graveside of Maggie Bateson once more. He looked just beyond it and saw how Brady and Stokes had removed the overgrowth to reveal the red stone of the adjacent plot – that of Janet Page.

The thinking time afforded by his long walk had done nothing to clarify the situation in Armstrong's mind. He looked into the empty grave, as if seeking inspiration; none was forthcoming. He then idled around aimlessly, looking at names on the graves that had stones, before arriving at the church door. Harry Stokes had briefed Armstrong on his discovery of the Janet Page grave from his inspection of the records inside but Cornelius decided to enter anyway.

The church was empty and dark, and despite the pleasant summer temperature outside, decidedly cool. Armstrong saw two books on a shelf under some notices to the right of the entrance. One was marked "Burial Records," the other "Visitors." Looking through the first, Cornelius flicked through a few pages to the year 1833: sure enough, beside the grave of Margaret Bateson was listed the name Janet Page. Both the deceased were listed as dying of "natural causes" and both were buried at six o'clock in the morning on the 29th January 1833.

Absentmindedly, Cornelius then glanced across at the second book that lay open for visitors to sign and add their comments and thoughts. About to turn away, he did a double take and the final entry on the page caught his eye. Someone had entered the words "A Dickens reader" and given an address of 37 Howard Place, Carlisle. According to the date column, the entry had been made the previous day. *Gridley, Chivery and now the reference to Dickens himself* – "There is coincidence and coincidence," Armstrong mumbled out loud and then self-consciously looked round to see if anyone had heard him. No one had – the church was empty.

As he came out of the gates, Cornelius managed to hop on a tram leading from Kingstown into the city. As Scotland Road rattled by, he couldn't help feeling that someone was now leaving him a path of breadcrumbs; leading him around the city as if to set him up for a fall at the completion of the trail. In one of his less lucid thoughts, the *Journal* reporter Jack Dixon even sprang to mind: *seeking a story and humiliating the local force into the bargain.*

The conductor calling the stop just over Eden Bridges put an end to such nonsense and the policeman jumped off and headed east. He walked the half-mile through the city centre and down Warwick Road to the elegant tree-lined Howard Place. On one side of the avenue were large detached villas while on the other, stood beautiful red-bricked town houses, whose bay windows stood out from their respective buildings in regimental fashion.

Cornelius didn't need to consult his pocket book – he wandered along the pavement until he stood in front of the stained-glass panelled door of number 37.

Looking up and down at the front elevation of the house, he admired its elegance: the door was flanked by inset columns, while above was an ornate canopy. The red brick fascia led the eye up three floors, all facilitated by twin sash windows to what appeared to be an attic room that nestled under a steep dormer pitch that protruded at right angles from the main roof.

The policeman now wondered if this might be an ill-judged decision that would only result in the owner – no doubt another member of the gentry – tearing a strip off him for wasting their time; worse still, if he turned out to be somehow connected to the Corporation or the Watch Committee. To counter the feelings of self-doubt, Armstrong reminded himself as he stood in front of the house that it would niggle away at him if he didn't follow up this line of enquiry, no matter how bizarre it seemed. He took a deep breath and pushed the white button at the centre of the large bell that was mounted on the right hand side of the door.

After a few seconds, he saw a distorted figure approaching through the stained glass. The door opened and Armstrong immediately thought he had been mistaken for someone else, as the butler casually said, "Good afternoon, sir, please come in, you are expected." The butler spoke with a slightly strange accent and stood aside to allow the bemused inspector through the vestibule and into the hall; he then showed the visitor along the passageway and through the final door on the right hand side. Before Cornelius had even followed him across the threshold, the butler announced, "Inspector Armstrong, sir," to whoever was inside.

The culprit revealed

Cornelius followed the butler into the room, at the far end of which, in front of the window sat an old man in a blue, wing-backed chair. The room, like the hallway, was sparsely furnished but the furniture and decor that was there was of the highest quality.

"Come in inspector," said the old man, gesturing for his guest to take one of the other two seats in the room. Then addressing the butler: "Would you organise some tea for us please, Michael? And take the inspector's hat and coat – I have a feeling we may be some time."

The butler obeyed his master and Cornelius complied with some bemusement. As Michael left the room, the old man again pointed towards the chair, "Please, please…" and then with a mischievous smile, "I take it you read a bit of Dickens?"

Armstrong was trying to clear his head and heard himself ask foolishly, "Mr. Gridley?"

"No, not really," said the old man, "but like dear old Gridley, no one would listen to me." He spoke with a croaky voice that clearly had a Carlisle foundation to it, but was occasionally betrayed by an incongruous lilt. "I hoped you wouldn't deny me a little bit of fun in my old age inspector?"

The detective was both satisfied that he had worked the sobriquet out and yet confused at the need for deception. He took a more serious tone, "That depends on whether you've been involved in the disturbances of various graves in the city recently."

The man looked hard at the policeman. "Two, I believe," he said at last.

"*With more to come?*" Cornelius finally sat down opposite the man, his instinct telling him that his investigation was coming to a conclusion. He looked closely at the man, who had a tanned, almost leathery face; his white, wiry hair blended into the starched antimacassar that hung behind his head. His hands had the same brownish hue as his face but were peppered with liver spots. But for all his unhealthy appearance the man was dressed immaculately in shirt, waistcoat, trousers and frockcoat that were clearly of the highest quality. Obviously proud of his appearance, the man wore a pale blue cravat, while a matching handkerchief peeped out of the top pocket of his coat.

Armstrong looked the man in the eye. "Tell me what you know."

"Before I do," he said, "there is someone else I think you should meet." He rang a little bell that stood on a small table beside his chair. A man entered the room.

The man: as immaculately dressed as his master but much younger with distinctive long, collar-length hair and a neatly manicured beard that looked as though it had been lightly painted on the lower half of his face. Armstrong felt himself starting to flush with anger at seeing the man he felt had been leading him by the nose through his investigation. Before he could voice his fury the old man spoke again.

"I think you are a very clever man, Inspector. I'm hoping that you will turn out to be a very fair one too. The operative word there of course is 'turn'. You see that is my name…Jacob Turn."

As Armstrong was distracted by the presence of the new arrival, it took a couple of seconds for the name to register, but when it did, his head snapped back towards his host and his piercing blue eyes widened in amazement. He sat forward in his chair, "*My God!* The brother of John Henry Turn,"

"Ah, I see it's not just fiction you read," said Jacob. "The very same; John and I were ordinary lads from an ordinary Carlisle family, but if Dickens ever wrote our story, no one would believe it."

Very deliberately, Jacob took a drink of water from a glass that sat on the small table. He then gestured towards the other man, "This is Nathanael Cooke and he is in my employment. Please do not judge him harshly Mr. Armstrong, everything he did, he did under my instruction."

"Pleased to meet you at last, sir," said Cooke offering a hand, "After learning so much about you I'm a great admirer of yours inspector."

Somewhat placated, but still confused Cornelius shook the man's hand and sat back down. "There is still a lot of explaining to do," he said.

Just then, Michael returned with a tray of tea and biscuits. Pouring three cups, he then left, closing the door behind him which somehow signified a long meeting was about to take place. Jacob took a sip of tea, followed by a deep breath and began his narrative.

"John was my older brother. He was born in 1815, when Britain was still at war with Napoleon. I came along four years later. Our mum and dad lived in Caldewgate, they were both handloom weavers – I don't think there was much else to do in those days, and sure enough, when we were old enough, we took up the same profession. We lost them both to the cholera epidemic in the early 1830s. John was seventeen at the time; I had just turned fourteen. There was no chance of anybody employing a couple of kids so John applied to the Overseer for the Poor to see if we could be supported by the parish. Not surprisingly he was unsuccessful, and we ended up in the workhouse." Jacob looked aimlessly past Armstrong, "If we felt hard done by beforehand, little did we know that our troubles were just beginning.

"The workhouse was run by a so-called gentleman by the grand name of Mr. Jeremiah Wednesbury and his wife Elizabeth." He spat the words out. "Two more villainous creatures you could not have the misfortune of meeting."

Armstrong looked at Turn with surprise, prompting the man to continue.

"John Henry was a good lad and as you've probably gathered, used to look out for me. When we ended up in that horrible place, it was John who tried to keep my spirits up by telling me that this was just a temporary arrangement. The poor lad was proved right, but he could never have predicted our eventual destiny.

"Despite our humble upbringing, our parents did their best to give us an education, teaching us to read and write. John in particular was a good scholar and when we started in the workhouse, Wednesbury cottoned on to John's skills and employed him as a sort of bookkeeper.

"All was well for the first six months or so, but then John stumbled upon some discrepancies in the registers of the poor souls unfortunate enough to be housed in that God-forsaken place... I can't remember the gist exactly…something about the number of people who *were* there and the number who *should* have been there.

"Being a young inquisitive lad, John looked deeper into it and found that records had not been properly altered following the deaths of people in the workhouse for a period of years. When he discovered a pattern that involved young, relatively fit women, his suspicions were aroused sufficiently to ask Wednesbury about the anomaly. This was his big mistake.

"Wednesbury first tried to fob him off with some cock-and-bull story but John kept an eye on what was going on and found that a man was visiting the workhouse regularly from Glasgow. He observed his visits and noted the timing was always around the time of one of the women dying. He wasn't sure how long it had been going on for, but it became quite noticeable in 1833. So much so, that John went back to Wednesbury to ask again about the pattern. The villain told him that he had an errand for him and me to carry out the following day, and once we returned, he would have a chat with him. Of course, that chat would never take place.

"The errand involved us going up to the cemetery. Wednesbury said he had promised the watchman use of some spades and shovels for grave digging. It was our job to deliver the tools; where the watchman would meet us at the paupers' burial site.

"I remember it as if it were yesterday. It was a sharp early autumn morning with thick dew covering any greenery; when we got there we found no one about, but our attention was drawn to a grave that lay empty beside a mound of earth that had been displaced.

"As if right on cue, just as we were looking into the grave, a constable appeared and claimed that we must have removed the body."

Cornelius Armstrong had listened patiently to that point. "How could he claim that when you didn't have the body?"

"That's a good question inspector – a question that was conveniently ignored along with several others at our trial. We were accused of robbing not only that grave, but also others at Stanwix and St. Cuthbert's.

"It was following a period when grave robbing and body snatching was quite widespread, especially in Scotland and the north of England. Villains would raid the graves of recently deceased persons and sell their bodies to scientists and doctors for dissection. Poor John and I never knew any of this of course at the time. We were just a couple of innocent young lads who were taken advantage of. They wouldn't listen to any of our arguments.

"We were found guilty in no time, and my beautiful brother who never harmed anyone in his short life, and who had turned eighteen in the meantime, was hanged. Because I was only fourteen at the time, I was deported to Australia for seven years' hard labour. Jacob paused for several seconds staring past Cornelius at nothing in particular. "Within twelve months I had lost my mother and father, and my brother; and I would then find myself on the other side of the world in a penal colony, smashing up rocks in the hot barren wastelands of Australia. I vowed every day and every night during that hell on earth to clear the names of John Henry Turn and his young brother Jacob."

Australia

"Hard labour? It's well named – *by God it was hard!*" Jacob was full of bitterness as he told his tale.

The young boy had naturally never been outside of the walls of Carlisle in his fourteen years and all of a sudden there he was, having been arrested, tried and convicted within six weeks; seen his brother hanged; and now herded onto a cattle train down to London and then dumped on one of the hulks anchored along the banks of the Thames.

The cruel hiatus in the nation's capital served as a foretaste of what the child was to experience in the months and years that were to follow. The hulks were old navy ships used to ease the burden on the overcrowded prisons; convicts would be crammed into the floating gaols as they waited to be assigned to one of the dozens of vessels that sailed between the northern and southern hemispheres.

Conditions were disgusting; if Jacob thought that the surroundings of the St. Mary's Workhouse were austere, they were palatial by comparison with the omnipresent stench and damp of the hulk. The ice-cold days were spent doing hard labour on the dockside or hacking through the ice in a futile attempt to dredge the river, while nights were spent chained to a bunk in the dark, cramped hold, listening to the incessant dripping of water onto the bare timber decks. When the dripping stopped the convicts knew that they would awaken to find stalactites hanging from the low ceiling.

Another young boy who joined the ship on the same day as Jacob was destined never to leave England – he succumbed to typhoid within a week on the disease-ridden vessel. By some miracle Jacob made it through the month that seemed like an eternity and was assigned to a convict ship that weighed anchor on another bitterly cold December morning in 1833.

Conditions on board were only marginally better that those experienced on the hulk. Young Turn – like many of his shipmates who had never been to sea before – constantly struggled to keep down the slop they were fed, as the ship bucked and dipped on the high sea. Three months into the six-month journey south, while Jacob was one of a group of convicts swabbing the deck, a crewman told him that young boys like him would be dropped off in Tasmania where the work was lighter than in New South Wales. In his bemused, frightened state, the youngster didn't understand a word the man said to him. Instead he simply peered towards the horizon in all directions, terrified as he could not see land anywhere.

He witnessed men being restrained in heavy irons, others being flogged, and the unfortunates who succumbed to rampant diseases tossed overboard. By the time they arrived on mainland Australia the human cargo had been reduced by a third, and those that were left were emaciated and suffering from one ailment or another.

It was because of such illness that Jacob never disembarked in Tasmania like most of his age group. Instead, he was shipped on to Botany Bay with the rest of the convicts where he was tended to by doctors on the quayside until he was judged fit enough and allocated to a work camp. The most hardened criminals were sent to special prisons or sites hundreds of miles from anywhere that made escape impossible. Jacob meanwhile, was assigned to the penal colony up country at Moreton Bay, three days journey in a cattle train.

Initially he worked as a servant to the settlers in the area but within eighteen months, he was assigned to the hard labour gangs. As the sun beat down on the scorched land, the fair-skinned Englishmen broke rocks under armed military guards. Jacob was wise enough to keep out of trouble in this harsh environment where punishments were brutal. If a convict was found to be feigning illness or avoiding his duties, the rest would be lined up to deter them from following suit as they witnessed their colleague receive fifty lashes with the cat o'nine tails. If one of the convicts was foolish enough to attempt an escape he would be lashed before being shackled in ankle irons and placed in the one of the chain gangs whose back-breaking task it was to excavate new roads in the hard, arid land.

Jacob would spend endless nights incarcerated in a small wooden hut behind the stockade, lying on his bunk trying to make sense of the bizarre injustice that had brought him to this God-forsaken place. Seven long years passed dominated by sun, dust and armies of mosquitoes, until the young man finally received his certificate of freedom in 1842. But with no family, no home and no money, what was he to do?

*

"Then fate finally looked kindly upon me Mr. Armstrong," said Jacob finally returning his gaze to his guest with a smile that developed into an involuntary cough rising from the old man's chest. Cornelius had sat gripped by his story for over an hour. Jacob took a sip of water and continued.

"When my seven years were up, I drifted back down south and landed a job with a mining company in New South Wales. I had only been with them for a couple of years when they discovered gold in the Blue Mountains. Many have read about the gold rush of 1851 but for those of us lucky enough to be there already, it was a case of getting as rich as you can as quick as you can. The stuff was dripping from the mountains like honey from a hive.

"I made enough money to start my own mining business – went from being a child criminal at fourteen to being a millionaire at thirty-five with a large mansion near the Bell River. Along the way, I expanded my modest education, gorging on Shakespeare and Dickens, collecting fine art and learning about Mozart and Beethoven. So you see we have bit in common, you and me," he added with a smile.

"It was the summer of 1850 when I met the most beautiful girl I had ever seen. Rosalind was the daughter of one of the wealthy timber barons up country near where we know today as Maryborough in Queensland. She came to New South Wales to teach at the local school; I was lucky enough to meet her at a friend's garden party one lovely afternoon. I couldn't take my eyes off her and, Lord knows why, but she seemed to like me too!

"We were married the following year as prospectors from all over the world descended on New South Wales in their quest for fame and mainly fortune.

"My life has been one of extremes Mr. Armstrong: for the first twenty five years it was hell; for the forty I then spent with Rosalind it was heaven. We were rich beyond all imagination but alas we weren't blessed with any children. So when Rosalind was taken from me five years ago, I decided to concentrate on the one unresolved issue that had niggled away at me for a lifetime – my desire for justice regarding my brother and me.

"It may seem like a waste of time to most people. Trying to right a wrong from seventy years earlier, twelve thousand miles away, when everyone had forgotten who or what was involved. But we all have our little demons Mr. Armstrong and mine kept telling me that I owed it to John Henry and myself to do whatever I could to clear our names before my own time was up.

"Rosalind had relatives in London who were solicitors and I approached them first to see if they could commission an investigation on my behalf. That's where young Nate here comes in." He indicated to Nathanael Cooke who had sat quietly opposite Cornelius throughout Jacob's narrative.

"It took quite a while for him to complete his enquiries and while he was doing so, I travelled back to England and made arrangements to purchase a property in my home city." He looked round the room, "it's fairly modest but more than serves its purpose.

"I must confess inspector, one of Nathanael's instructions was to identify a good trustworthy officer of the law who would carry out his own investigation – perhaps with a little help – and corroborate my version of events. Forgive me Mr. Armstrong but Nate here found out a lot about you too, including your own taste in literature.

"The one thing neither of us anticipated of course was the appearance of the young American. Nate ran into him by accident in the church and learned in conversation about his background and his acquaintance with your good self. You see the staggering coincidence is that I knew his grandfather old Reverend Woodrow; he used to visit us at the workhouse. Lovely chap he was" – mentioning the workhouse prompted darker thoughts – "unlike that scoundrel that ran the place: masquerading as a fine upstanding member of the Presbyterian community." Turn's old face contorted in disgust, "Makes me sick just thinking about it."

Jacob looked earnestly at his guest: "I don't have long left inspector so I decided to return to England myself in order to expose – or should I say unearth – the truth. Without ever knowing it, you haven't let me down yet Mr. Armstrong, I hope you won't now."

Exhuming the truth

"I don't understand," said Cornelius. The first part of Jacob Turn's story had been compelling but what about the here and now? "How can robbing graves today clear yours and your brother's names from seventy years ago?"

Jacob threw his head back and gave a cackling laugh that dissolved into a throaty, almost uncontrollable cough. He composed himself after a few seconds with the aid of another sip of water before answering, "There *were* no bodies Inspector, at least not in the graves! You see, John Henry and I weren't the guilty parties," – his tone was even – "Wednesbury and his wife were.

"John had the misfortune of stumbling on their little sideline of poisoning young single occupants of the workhouse; mainly young women with no relatives and no dependents. Who would miss them in a day and age where disease and death was rife? People outside the workhouse didn't want to know, and even those inside were oblivious and disinterested in anything other than their own living hell.

"When I returned to Carlisle after all these years Inspector, I couldn't resist visiting the places I once knew as a child. One such place was the gaol near the station." Jacob's eyes began to tear up as he recalled the final days he had with his brother, "When we were locked in that awful place, awaiting our fate, John told me what he had discovered. Wednesbury and his wife were poisoning the women and then having their bodies transported up to Edinburgh and Glasgow where they were sold on the black market. He then bribed the appropriate people to dig a fake grave and falsify the records at the various graveyards.

"They must have been at it for years before the Anatomy Act was passed the previous year. But of course that didn't stop the scoundrel carrying on his villainy and then blaming two young lads who didn't know any better, when he was found out. He claimed we had been robbing graves for years and had continued doing so for profit. What profit? If we made any money doing anything, why would be in the workhouse? And we were kids for God's sake, how could we have been at it for years?

"The truth is inspector we didn't steal any bodies because there were no bodies to steal, neither in 1833 or today.

"Now that there is a Court of Appeal in this wonderful country I have spent the last few months with my solicitors preparing my case – I hope it will be heard before the year is out. Having investigated the case yourself inspector, I was rather hoping a man of your standing would support it."

"I am a young detective with limited influence Mr. Turn," said Cornelius with some uncertainty.

"Lizzie Meggs, Elsie Grimes, Maggie Bateson, Janet Page, Lilly Carrick and Cissy Henderson. They are names that have been imprinted on my mind ever since John told me the story the night before he was hanged. I know the names and the locations – how do you think young Nathanael here knew where to dig?"

Armstrong glanced across at the investigator and then back again to Turn. After some thought he said, "The names you give are those that I found at the workhouse and in the ledgers at the various cemeteries. I suppose if what you are telling me is true, all of the graves will be empty?"

"That's quite right Inspector, that's why I asked Nate to just dig two of the empty graves and leave the others to the authorities." The old man sat forward in his chair and looked at the policeman earnestly, "I tell you now Mr. Armstrong, if there is anything in any one of those graves, I will build a scaffold myself in front of the town hall and hurl myself off it."

Cornelius was full of admiration for the old man's tenacity. "Well let's hope it doesn't come to that. You've made a very compelling case Mr. Turn," then turning to the other man, "and I must confess to being more impressed than offended at your work Mr. Cooke. He tweaked the horns of his moustache as he contemplated what he had learned that afternoon. At last he said "I always pride myself on doing the right thing; not necessarily the easy thing or the popular thing, but the right thing. And it seems to me that the right thing to do on this occasion is to restore the good names of John and Jacob Turn."

It was early evening before Jacob had completed his story; too late for Cornelius to speak to Henry Baker who would have left for the day, and too late to cancel the uniforms who would have been assigned to cemetery duty. So Inspector Armstrong left, advising Jacob that he would brief his chief constable and return with news the following day.

*

Cornelius was sitting at his desk just after eight o'clock when Henry Baker arrived. Armstrong gave the chief constable a few minutes before ambling down the corridor. The door was open and Henry was behind the desk preparing to read some papers he had taken out the drawer. Armstrong knocked on the door frame. Baker's forehead creased as he looked up to see his Inspector standing there. "News?" he asked hopefully.

"News," repeated the detective, closing the door behind him.

He informed the chief constable of the extraordinary events of the previous day and the even more extraordinary tale Jacob Turn had to tell. Baker was as astounded as Armstrong had been at the unlikely tale and sat in silence trying to take it all in. "You've had longer to think about this than I have Cornelius," he said at last, "what's your opinion?"

Armstrong took a deep breath, "I think there are two alternatives. We can do nothing, having *solved* the case, so to speak, and warn Jacob and his man off any repeat performance, that will only succeed in unsettling the public. Alternatively we make representation to the Watch Committee and the Corporation and support Jacob's cause."

"And dig up the other graves you mean?" asked Baker uncertainly.

"Precisely." Armstrong's tone was even.

Baker then asked a question he already knew the answer to, "And which course do you think we should take?"

"You and I both know the answer to that Henry; we also know it is the right thing to do. Besides Jacob is now a very rich man who has travelled twelve thousand miles in his old age to right this wrong. Shooing him away will only strengthen his resolve, which will see him throw more money at the problem causing all sorts of embarrassment and discomfort along the way."

"Very well," agreed Baker, "let's get the Watch Committee together for starters and see what they have to say."

*

The committee sat around a large oval oak table at the town hall. There was much grumbling amongst the elderly members who wondered aloud what was so urgent as to pull them away from their bridge and their golf; what's more, George Sowerby had also promised to help his wife tidy the garden up with it being such a nice day.

Chief Constable Baker and Inspector Armstrong sat before them not particularly looking forward to reciting the fanciful tale, let alone putting their proposal of further digging to prove the old man's claims.

During the Inspector's recital there were plenty of derogatory snorts, but as Baker had done following Armstrong's narrative, the committee sat in silence at its conclusion trying to comprehend what they had just learned. Armstrong meanwhile prepared himself for the predictable questions and lame reasons for not pursuing the course of action he was proposing.

"Surely sacred ground has still been disturbed," said one member.

"I think any fair-minded person would agree it was with good reason, sir," said Cornelius. "After all, there are no actual bodies in the graves, and Turn believed that by demonstrating such, he stood more chance of getting the authorities to accept his story, rather than simply making representation that would be laughed off as being absurd."

"Surely pursuing such a course of action would sully the name of this Wednesday chap?" asked another. The question rather died on his lips as he realised that if he was guilty he didn't deserve to have a good name.

"Wednes*bury*," corrected Armstrong. He continued, "This isn't about proving his guilt, it's about proving the Turn brothers' innocence. I don't doubt that there is any chance of finding evidence to incriminate Wednesbury and any associates, but the fact that there is no evidence against Jacob and his brother either should lead them to be pardoned."

Cornelius held up the newspapers from the day featuring the story, "If anyone were to read the case, they would find that no bodies were ever recovered. What's more the then-vicar of St. Cuthbert's Church, told the newspaper that there were no signs of any disturbances in his churchyard, despite it being listed as one of the desecrated sites. But then he was never called as a witness in the boys' trial.

"Two other issues need to be considered: first, it was accepted by all that these so-called grave robbing incidents took place during the night under the cover of darkness. How then could the brothers commit such crimes when they lived in the workhouse that locks its doors at six o'clock until seven the next morning? *They couldn't get out to commit these, or any other crimes!*"

Some members of the committee had never met Armstrong before – not that that had deterred them hitherto from expressing their disapproval at his appointment – but they all seemed suitably impressed with the young detective's authoritative tone and his sense of justice. One by one, expressions gradually changed and heads began to nod in unison until the Chairman Herbert Underwood spoke at the end of Armstrong's presentation.

"Well inspector, you provide a very compelling case on behalf of Mr. Turn, and whether he is innocent or not, it is fairly clear that you have solved this matter that was concerning us greatly." He then addressed his colleagues, "Could I propose that we reflect on what Inspector Armstrong has told us and invite this Jacob Turn to meet with us before the week is out. If we believe he and his late brother have been wronged we can then make representation to the Corporation and the church to seek permission to dig up the graves in order to either prove or disprove his case."

"I second the proposal," came a voice from the far end of the table.

A vote was taken with the majority of members raising their hands without hesitation in support of Underwood's proposal; the few that remained thought for a few seconds and couldn't come up with justifiable alternative, so they gradually joined their colleagues making it a unanimous decision.

The meeting broke up with the two policemen extremely satisfied with the outcome: Armstrong had presented a concise yet cogent case, and Baker was pleased that the committee had finally seen his inspector in action which could only help in easing their concerns about the younger man's capabilities and his own decision-making.

Cornelius wasted no time in re-tracing his steps from the previous day to visit Jacob Turn.

"Thank you inspector," said the old man upon hearing the news, "I was confident I could rely on your support and you haven't let me down." He told Armstrong that he intended for his solicitor to travel up from London for the meeting and if things went as planned, he would stay to witness "...the digging," as Jacob termed it. He also informed the policeman that his investigator, Nathanael Cooke, had returned to the capital following the completion of his work.

As Cornelius rose to leave he said, "On a lighter note it occurred to me that I arranged to meet with Professor Wilson upon his return to Carlisle. Given that you told me you knew his grandfather, I'm sure he would love to meet you."

"Ah, the young American, of course," said Jacob. "Why don't you invite him round here and we'll all have dinner? My faithful companion Michael has been with me for years and he came over here with me – he is also a wonderful cook."

"I know Woodrow will like that," said Armstrong. The two shook hands, "I will see you later in the week in front of the Watch Committee."

"I'll look forward to it," said Jacob with keenness in his eyes that hadn't been there during their previous meeting. "And thank you Cornelius, I really can't thank you enough."

*

Woodrow Wilson arrived back in Carlisle full of enthusiasm after his cycling tour of the Lakes. He met briefly with Cornelius and told him about accompanying Mr. and Mrs. Wood, whom he had met on the boat coming over; how they had visited Cockermouth and Grasmere in researching William Wordsworth; and how there was simply so much to do and see, he had resolved to come back to this beautiful place.

When Armstrong told him about Jacob Turn and how he met Wilson's grandfather, it served to complete the American's excitement about his family pilgrimage. Cornelius then arranged to meet Woodrow at his hotel the night before he left for home and they would walk the half mile or so down Warwick Road to meet Jacob, appropriately enough, passing the Reverend Woodrow's former house along the way.

The evening proved fascinating for the three men. They represented different continents and yet this quiet northern city, with its checkered history, provided the common link between the three. Wilson was fascinated about Jacob's encounters with his grandfather, Reverend Thomas Woodrow, and Turn were equally interested in the professor's life and career in America – a place which for all his wealth, he had never visited.

Jacob had been in a good mood before his guests had even arrived as that afternoon had seen the last grave dug out, following his meeting with Cornelius three weeks earlier. In the intervening time, he had met with the Watch Committee, achieved the appropriate permission from the local authorities and been present, accompanied by his solicitor at the three diggings at Carlisle and Stanwix cemeteries and St. Cuthbert's Churchyard.

As Jacob had predicted, there were no bodies in any of the graves: neither the ones marked as being disturbed in 1833, nor the ones immediately adjacent which in theory, should have been occupied. His solicitor had therefore returned to London immediately to progress his appeal against his conviction.

Like everyone who had heard Jacob's mysterious story to date, Woodrow Wilson was transfixed by the narrative. "I know the United States has nothing to do with the matter my dear Jacob," he said, "but I happen to know the Ambassador to Great Britain; I don't think it would do any harm to ask him to exert whatever influence he has along the corridors of power."

Jacob found himself moved by such kindness, "Thank you Woodrow," and then turning to Cornelius he added, "In meeting such good people it restores my faith in humanity. I have had a long, hard life and experienced incredible hardship and injustice along with good fortune and great happiness in equal measure. I'm now getting very tired gentlemen, as my life draws to an end; I just hope between us we can right this wrong before I'm laid to rest."

December 1918

As the torrential rain pounded against the side of the carriage and the train rattled through northern Cumberland towards Carlisle, President Wilson peered expectantly out of the window.

It was a journey he had been looking forward to for some time and; having travelled to Europe to attend the peace conference in Paris, he was determined to make what he termed his "pilgrimage of the heart" to his darling mother's home city.

He had once sat in a small house in the city and listened to the remarkable story of man who had experienced incredible triumphs and tragedies in his long life. In the twenty-two years since his last visit to the city, Woodrow Wilson had himself experienced triumphs and tragedies that could never have been imagined nor predicted, as he sat listening the to the old man.

Six years after his visit to Carlisle his popularity and oratory skills had seen him advance from being professor to president of Princeton University. The health issues that dogged him ten years earlier however affected him again when he suffered another stoke in 1906. Not that that stopped officials from the Democratic Party from badgering him into becoming governor of New Jersey as the first decade of the new century ended. Then, two years later, the man who once wandered the streets of Carlisle in virtual anonymity was successfully nominated as the party's candidate for the top job and was duly elected as the 28th President of the United States.

Re-elected for a second term in 1916, the President maintained a stance of neutrality as war raged in Europe, until American merchant vessels were sunk by German submarines in the Atlantic, and Germany tried to enlist Mexico as a fighting ally. Eighteen months later, the war was over and the President was travelling to London to stay with the King and Queen before crossing the Channel to the Peace Conference in Versailles.

But beforehand, he made it known to his Royal hosts that he intended to travel north to visit Carlisle on a personal, unofficial visit. The King kindly offered him use of his own train. The President of the United States travelling on the Royal Train therefore was unlikely to be kept secret and the city was abuzz with excitement.

The president stepped down from the train onto the red-carpeted platform, as the rain hammered down on the large glass roof of the station, to be greeted by the mayor and a line of local dignitaries who escorted the presidential party to the square outside. As they appeared an enormous roar went up from the thousands of people that had braved the weather to catch a glimpse of Mr. and Mrs. Wilson.

The first lady turned to the mayor and said, "I can't believe it; it seems as though the whole population has turned out on such a day as this. With all of the dripping umbrellas, all manoeuvring for position, it's like entering a forest of giant toadstools!"

The President removed his top hat as he acknowledged the crowd and he and his wife risked becoming soaked as they continually waved to the cheering onlookers before his aides ushered him into his limousine that was part of the ten-vehicle motorcade that pulled away and headed for the

Crown and Mitre Hotel. Despite the weather, their route continued to be lined by oilskins and black umbrellas. "So much for a discrete, private visit!" commented the president to his wife as they waved to the massive crowds.

Once inside the hotel, another line of dignitaries awaited their introduction to the president. Mr. Wilson shook the hand of each one as they were introduced to him by the mayor. As he completed the ritual, he was about to be ushered to the dining room for a reception when a man in a knee-length overcoat and black Homberg, standing by the main entrance in the foyer, caught his eye, forcing him to do a double take. He had walked past him upon entering the hotel without noticing him but now he paused before fully recognising the horned moustache and piercing blue eyes of his old acquaintance.

"Cornelius!" he exclaimed walking over and offering a hand. "I nearly missed you!"

"Hello Mr. President," said the policeman, "it's nice to see you again. I'm amazed you remember me."

"Oh I could never forget the kindness you showed me when I visited Carlisle all those years ago."

"Much has changed sir, if you don't mind me saying. I never thought when we met then that I would be in the company of a future president."

"Nor did I!" said Wilson. The two laughed like old friends as bemused dignitaries and concerned Secret Servicemen looked on. "Tell me," said the president, "whatever happened regarding our mutual Australian friend?"

"It was a happy ending, I'm pleased to report," said Cornelius. He explained how Jacob's case was finally heard by the Court of Appeal and he was completely exonerated of any wrongdoing. As the court could not deal with those already dead, the old man continued his campaign until he achieved a posthumous Royal Pardon for his brother. "Jacob finally died a few years into the new century and – as per his request – was laid to rest alongside his brother John Henry in the paupers' burial site at the cemetery."

"What a wonderful story, Cornelius. I'm so pleased to hear such a heart-warming tale when we've all suffered so much over the past few years."

"Forgive me Mr. President," said a voice from behind – it was his chief of staff, "but we really are on a tight schedule."

"Of course, of course," said Mr. Wilson. The visit to Carlisle was only due to be for a few hours before heading back south. He turned again to Armstrong, "I hope we can steal a further chat before I leave," he said.

"It may be possible, sir. I'm on duty so I will be following your party around during your tour."

Inspector Armstrong maintained his station while the president signed the freemen's roll and his party enjoyed some light refreshment before being driven to Annettwell Street to see the site of the Congregational Church, while the Salvation Army band played the Star Spangled Banner.

From there the president's motorcade – laden with aides and Secret Service personnel – proceeded to Cavendish House on Warwick Road, the house his grandfather built almost a century earlier. Flags adorned the pillars and Mr. Wilson again paused on the steps and raised his hat to hundreds more cheering onlookers. He paused briefly trying to remember where exactly he had dined with Cornelius and Jacob Turn during the final night of his previous visit to the city. He knew it was close by but couldn't quite get his bearings in relation to his grandfather's house.

Ever since the McKinley assassination, security was always tight around the President and his secret servicemen never allowed him long to linger in any one place. Local police were always kept at arms' length and although they followed at a discrete distance, Inspector Armstrong had his men positioned where the crowds could be observed and controlled. He observed the president's security men encouraging him into his grandfather's old home and hovering around the entrance until he re-emerged.

From the Reverend Woodrow's old house, the president's whistle-stop tour continued at the Congregational Church, where a service was held in his honour. The dark clouds eased a little as Mr. Wilson alighted and he again caught a fleeting glance of Inspector Armstrong who had walked the short distance up Warwick Road. Unable to get close enough to speak, the two men gave each other a smile and a nod as the president entered the church.

Reverend Edward Booth addressed the congregation and welcomed his distinguished visitor, "I feel great pride that the great and honoured leader of the American people should have left the company of kings and set aside important functions to travel to this border city in which his mother was born, to attend as a humble worshiper in the church over which his grandfather once presided. Such action reveals his character. It is a great spectacle for the world.

"Mr. President, two-thirds of your name belongs here as the words Thomas Woodrow were inscribed on the church roll ninety-eight years ago." The pastor went on to give a history of the Woodrow family, culminating in them immigrating to America, and then invited the president to say a few words.

It had never been Mr. Wilson's intention to speak or indeed to receive such accolades but after a moment's hesitation, he agreed and lightened the tone a little by informing the congregation how his visit – or anything else for that matter -- might never have happened. He explained, "I will tell you how nearly this ceremony came to not taking place. My mother was playing on a rope on the ship while sailing for America and a sudden lurch nearly threw her overboard. She apparently swung far out over the water, but luckily for me she hung on and wasn't drowned."

The congregation laughed and shortly after, the service ended with the playing of the national anthem. The cheering crowd never decreased as the presidential party was then whisked off to the cathedral and then back to the Crown and Mitre before the four-hour visit ended with the motorcade easing its way back to the station.

Cornelius Armstrong was one of scores of people on the platform as the president and the first lady made their way back along the red carpet to the Royal Train. Again Mr. Wilson caught a glimpse of him and raised his hat in recognition one last time.

Looking through the windows of the train, the people on the platform could see those on board taking their seats. Then suddenly, and much to the surprise and confusion of his entourage, the president himself got up and started to walk back along the carriage towards the door. His Secret Service agents shuffled about in the background as Mr.

Wilson slid down the window and leant out scouring the crowd. The onlookers responded with another loud cheer but they didn't realise that the President was not seeking an encore; he was looking for someone in particular.

Finally he found his man amongst the sea of faces and waved at Cornelius Armstrong to come forward. The people on the platform were as bemused as the policeman as he stepped forward and leaned in to hear what Woodrow Wilson had to say to him above the din of the crowd.

"I've just remembered Cornelius…" said the President with a smile, "how is to the piano playing coming along?"

The Devil's Porridge

Another night in 'Blue Lugs'

"Aw, not again!" Ernie Jeffers, the landlord of *The Joiners' Arms* in Caldewgate, looked out over his bar to the far corner of his pub. For the third night this week, things were kicking off. One of the trestle tables had been disturbed and a couple of tankards had clanged against the flagged flooring of the modest pub. The incident acted as the trigger for another night of rowdiness.

A group of railway navvies had been occupying the table when another group had started shoving each other close by with the inevitable consequence. Before long, both groups were going at it without a care for their own safety, or anyone else's.

At an adjoining table were Reuben Hanks and a group of his friends. When the two groups of navvies crashed on to Hanks's table the scuffle became an all-out pub brawl with the local men being dragged in. When his drink was upset, Reuben's friend Barney Edwards – "Bog Rat" to the group, due to his appalling personal hygiene and general dirty habits – leapt up and planted a right hand on the jaw of the man who had been pushed towards him.

He quickly recovered and lunged at Bog Rat who, much to Reuben's surprise, dodged his oncoming assailant with a neat side-step.

"Obviously not drunk enough!" shouted Tommy Lloyd across at Hanks. Lloyd – another of the group – had also seen Bog Rat's deftness and read Hanks's thoughts. Each night the friends were together, Bog Rat would invariably end up drunk and have to be virtually carried home by his friends.

Before Hanks could respond to Lloydy's quip, he felt a stray punch to the back of the head and turned to face two others who were squabbling. Hanks had a muscular build and in his fury he floored one with a big right hand and elbowed the other almost in the same movement. The second man felt his front teeth splinter as he fell backwards towards the floor. As he did so his legs splayed and caused the chain reaction of tripping someone close by, who in turn fell into another table, which inevitably prompted its occupants to join in the fight.

By this time shouts and cries filled the whole pub. Ernie sent his wife Audrey out the back way to get the police. As she left the bar area a tankard flew across the room and caught Ernie a glancing blow drawing blood from one of his large blue ears in the process. The landlord had witnessed a few brawls in his time – even before the influx of railway workers – but this was shaping up to be one of the worst, certainly in his pub.

Reuben Hanks had been knocked to the floor by this point; he aimed a kick with the sole of his boot at the side of the knee of the man who put him there. His aggressor let out a loud yelp as his leg buckled under him. It was a chaotic scene with blows, kicks, wooden stools and tankards raining in from all angles. Knuckles slammed flesh, knees rammed guts and shins whacked thigh muscles.

Most of the protagonists were sporting cuts, gashes and bruises as the fight raged on. One of the navvies who originated the melee even clambered up onto the bar and hurled himself into the heaving mass below him, as if it were all some sort of choreographed performance. The crunching noise his action made temporarily drowned out the general scuffling din of the disorganised wrestlers and back street pugilists. Men pushed, jostled and grabbed at each other's clothing.

Danny McKay – another of Reuben's group – was pulled to one side by one of the brawlers, almost as if the stranger felt he wasn't seeing much of the action. Danny responded to the man's actions by driving his forehead directly into his face. There was a crunch of cartilage and nasal bones, and as McKay drew away, it seemed the man's nose had adopted a new position. Blood spirted out as he spat on the floor. As he sank to his knees he instinctively reached down to find a piece of broken glass under his palm. In one movement he picked it up and made an upward lunge at Danny's face. McKay managed to dodge the weight of the main thrust but failed to avoid the makeshift weapon completely as it grazed his neck just above his collar. He cursed as, off balance, he appeared to be sucked unwillingly into the crowd of arms and legs.

McKay's friend Willie Tyson had tried to sneak out the back way but had been grabbed by his thick blonde locks and dragged back into where the action was. As he was dragged from behind, he was caught by a flailing fist square on the jaw. He growled angrily and lashed out with his foot. His kick caught someone in the groin and the high pitched squeal momentarily distracted some of the fighters.

Reuben was breathing hard and finding it difficult in the fuggy atmosphere; blood leaked from his nostrils, dribbled round his mouth and caught in the thick stubble on his chin. Two men were squaring up to him when he reached behind him and by chance grabbed hold of the leg of a stool that had been shattered against the back of someone. He swung it, backhand, in the general direction of his opponents. It swiped across the face of one snapping his head back and sending him to the floor; then with a forehand reverse, he managed to propel the other in the same direction. The two dropped with a clatter onto the hard, dusty floor, muck and sawdust billowing outward and upward at their impact.

Further up the road at the Irish Gate Tavern, Police Constables, Joe Brady, Tommy Gibson and Harry Stokes had just broken up a disturbance. They had calmed the situation down and were leaving.

"Bloody hell'"" said Brady to his two colleagues, "when are these blokes going to learn? How long's this nonsense been going on for anyway?"

Before either one of the policemen could answer, their colleague Bobby Green spotted them from across the street. "Down to the *Joiners'* lads!" he shouted, "it's kicked off down there!" There was a middle-aged woman scampering along trying to keep up with PC Green. "Knocking seven bells out of one another they are!" she shouted, as if to emphasise the urgency.

In the *Joiners' Arms* meanwhile, there was no let-up. Two dozen men were punching, gouging and swearing at one another; it was as though no one knew or cared whose side each was on. Moreover, they appeared to have completely overlooked the trivial incident that started the whole thing off ten minutes earlier.

One of the navvies drew a knife and started swiping at a man near him; the blade ripped his shirt as he leaped back in terror to avoid the weapon. Unchecked the knife-wielding maniac would have done untold damage and realising this, three of his own colleagues moved to restrain him. This gave his would-be victim a free hit and he duly obliged with a left, right combination that loosened the aggressor's grip on his weapon and it clattered to the floor.

As the knife was kicked out of harm's way, the men who were holding him seemed satisfied that it was a fair fight once more and released him to resume hostilities with his opponent. The two snarled at one another and instinctively lunged forward for more, while the others turned to find someone new to fight with.

Like many by this point, Danny McKay was fighting simply for survival against people he neither knew, nor had any issues with. An uppercut had knocked him back on his heels at one point and the jostling from an adjacent brawl had sent him spinning into the one hitherto undisturbed table, in the opposite corner to where the disturbance had started.

All of a sudden, the distinctive high pitch of a policeman's whistle could be heard above the raucous din of smashing glass and cheering brawlers. The approaching noise appeared to calm and even quieten the perpetrators inside the pub. Within a minute four uniformed policemen burst through the doors with their truncheons drawn. They didn't need them: the protagonists had stopped fighting and they now assumed an air of compliance, as if their impending arrest was all part of the natural process.

Behind the uniforms, their superior filled the doorway. His long brown knee-length coat and black bowler hat gave him an authoritative air; one that immediately commanded the attention of those present. His facial glow was evidence of his excursions in keeping up with his men as they ran down Bridge Street towards "Blue Lugs," but his horned moustache remained immaculately undisturbed.

Inspector Cornelius Armstrong scanned the room of now almost statuesque fighters. All around them was strewn glass, metal and timber. The sawdust that covered the flags was congealed through a combination of beer and blood. At first glance it looked like one of the worst incidents of its kind he had witnessed in recent years.

Armstrong saw Reuben Hanks and his friends in various guises of aggressor and victim. With a barely discernible motion of the head, he signalled for Hanks to disappear out the back way. Almost in the same movement he addressed his men, "Get this lot out of here and back to the station."

Nothing to worry about

The murder seems to have no political connection, although it is significant that the murder occurred in the capital of one of the two states Austria annexed without any regard to the wishes of the other Great Powers of Europe. When the time comes, the death of Franz Joseph [Ferdinand's father] will let loose or give fresh vitality to that which is now kept in check by the Emperor's personal influence and authority, and the struggle between Russia and Germany will become keener than ever.

Cornelius Armstrong put down the *Carlisle Journal* on 30th June 1914 as his housekeeper Mrs. Isabella Wheeler entered with his breakfast tray. It had been another late night at the station, after helping deal with the numerous arrests.

As Mrs. Wheeler put down the tray, her eye fell on the open newspaper.

"Oh, I was reading that earlier, sir," she said, "poor young man, and his lovely wife as well, if you please."

"Yes, there are some terrible people in this world I'm afraid Mrs. Wheeler," said Cornelius.

"I don't know what this daft world is coming to," mumbled the housekeeper, almost to herself as she turned to leave, "thank goodness we're kept well out of it."

Isabella Wheeler's view was representative of the average person in June and early July of 1914; the assassination of a man no one had heard of, more than a thousand miles away registered little as people went about their daily business.

They were more interested in the national stories: Ireland, labour unrest, the Women's Suffrage Movement.

Locally, it was the first of these issues that occupied most of Inspector Armstrong's professional time. Not so much the political issues on the island itself but its male emigrants who had found their way to the mainland looking for work on the railways, and in the docks of Liverpool and Glasgow. The last four years had been blighted by strike action throughout Britain and Ireland, and as the industrial action affected the big cities, navvies would make their way to Carlisle to escape the trouble and find casual work locally. Irish workers came to the city in their droves, as the national and local on-again, off-again disputes seemed to continue indefinitely.

This cycle of disruption and uncertainty had caused Armstrong and his men plenty of work over the years; the citizens were finding their Irish cousins to be hard workers and even harder drinkers. The pubs of Carlisle had never had it so good as the, many railway navvies, with plenty of disposable income, sought to dispose as much of it as possible in the nearest hostelry.

The problem for Armstrong and his men was that the navvies' reckless approach to their leisure time would invariably degenerate into drunkenness and violence. The station diary was full of incidents to that effect, particularly in Caldewgate – the Irish quarter of the city – but also in Botchergate, Wapping and Kingstown. The few cells situated at the back of the station were constantly occupied, and the governor of the county gaol, Geoffrey Lyons, found himself regularly imposed upon to accommodate the latest group of ruffians.

Not that the city itself had escaped the countrywide insurgency. The worst incident Cornelius could remember was during the national railway strike when a riot broke out at Citadel Station. Armstrong mustered as many men as he could in an effort to control the mob of striking workers, who had gathered in the beautiful square outside the station. The uniforms were pelted with flying bricks and bottles for their trouble.

If anything, the situation had become gradually worse over the past three years, and there were often times when Armstrong found himself doing little detective work; in its place would be peacekeeping activities and the seemingly endless logging in and out of various ne'er-do-wells as his uniformed colleagues were stretched to breaking point. The previous night's events were a good example.

Armstrong had been called out by one of his Bobbies and asked to assist in more disturbances in Caldewgate. First, there had been a relatively minor disturbance at the *Irish Gate Tavern* before a more serious fight had broken out at *The Globe*; then the men got the call from *The Joiners' Arms* – "Blue Lugs" to every local – where a full-scale riot had broken out. Clearing the pub and transporting the ruffians back to the station took two hours and four journeys for the police wagon. When the drunkards were all logged in, they were crammed into the overcrowded cells at the police station where they spent what was left of the night sleeping off their activity.

Usually, Cornelius was an avid reader of the local and national press and as such, was normally well-informed about national and international matters. During this most important of months however, this seemingly never-ending routine of breaking up drunken mobs, arresting them and locking them up, acted as a distraction from the machinations going on in London and on mainland Europe.

Like most people he was unaware of the various alliances between Germany and Austria-Hungary, Serbia and Russia, Russia and France, Britain and Belgium. As the month of July raced by, the commitments made by each country to support their respective allies – commitments that were initially designed and developed to prevent conflict – were the very mechanism by which each country was dragged inexorably towards a continental war, as first Vienna, supported by Germany declared war on Serbia. They in turn appealed to their Russian allies who in turn drew in France.

The first inkling the policeman had of Britain's involvement came when he received a telegram from his cousin, Sergeant George Armstrong, of the Border Regiment. Sergeant Armstrong had been accompanying the Territorial Battalion to their annual camp in Wales.

RETURNING EARLY STOP BEING MOBILISED
END
G

Forty-eight hours later, on the evening of what had been a blazing August day, George was sitting in *The Board* on the corner of Castle Street with his cousin discussing the impending crisis.

"Do you think this will go all the way?" asked Cornelius.

"Well, it looks that way," said George. "The word is that if the Germans attack the French through Belgium, we'll be dragged into it." Sergeant Armstrong was a veteran of the

Boer War some years earlier and didn't seem too concerned at the prospect. "Even if we are pulled into it, everyone seems pretty confident. Should all be over by Christmas they reckon."

Within days Britain was at war and jingoistic marches down Lowther Street and English Street provided some light relief for the people of the city as it conjured up apocryphal tales of the great Victorian campaigns that saw our lads defeating all those nasty fuzzy-wuzzies. But as the soldiers were waved off, this somehow felt different. Cornelius himself had lost his father – a corporal with the local regiment – during one of the foreign wars. As he watched one of the parades, he noted that there were no glittering squadrons of cavalrymen and regimental bands on this occasion; instead there were rows and rows of young men in drab khaki, with mechanized vehicles bringing up the rear. He looked around the thousands of smiling faces and thought that no one else seemed to share his feeling of foreboding.

As the crowds turned away and wandered home, they were soon to find their enthusiasm waning as within weeks they were being affected by food shortages and reduced working hours. Frustrations were compounded by base prejudice against the Irish who were seen by many as taking local jobs by day, and causing social disorder by night.

Predominant amongst the Irish visitors were Sean O'Doyle and Michael McGinty. Ardent Unionists from Antrim, the two had travelled up and down the northwest of England and throughout southwest Scotland, working on the railways and in the docks. They had found work as far apart as Stranraer and Liverpool – and many places in between – and as Carlisle was a good halfway point between the two extremes, O'Doyle and McGinty regularly gravitated towards the city between jobs.

Both were big men; McGinty especially was a mountain of a man and ideal for the heavy manual work demanded of navvies. The other benefit of being such a size was the rewards that could be gained from the brutal pastime of bare-knuckle fighting. McGinty proved himself a skilled exponent of the illegal sport back home, regularly winning contests in the seedy back halls of Antrim and Belfast. It was at such a gathering where he met O'Doyle and the two had been close ever since.

When they came to the mainland in May 1914, as well as scouring for work, O'Doyle wasted no time in making underground contacts that would be receptive to arranging such contests that invariably rewarded the participants well, and created considerable profit for the organisers from the illegal betting that inevitably accompanied such an event.

By the summer of 1915 the two Antrim men found themselves in Carlisle once more struggling to find any meaningful work. The timing of their arrival could not have worked out better for them however, as a crisis on the Western Front was inadvertently about to bring the city and its surrounding hinterlands to the nation's attention.

Suffering and suffrage

By the spring of 1915, the Border Regiment was slogging it out on the Western Front. Sergeant George Armstrong hastily wrote home to his cousin:

Dear Cornelius,

How I long to see you and the old place once more. I can't begin to tell you how bad things are here. We live from day to day, hour to hour in unspeakable fear, sloshing about in waterlogged, collapsing trenches in this incessant muddy rain, with meagre rations to keep us going. The danger of death or mutilation by shell or mortar fire, hand grenade or sniper's bullet is ever-present day and night. To see bodies being split down the middle and heads being blown off is commonplace. I thought I'd seen it all in South Africa but nothing can compare with this hell on earth.

Please pray for me don't tell my mother, for I know it would worry her so.

Your loving cousin,
George

Cornelius Armstrong sat in his chair staring blankly at the letter; the guilt felt by the policeman was palpable, knowing that there was nothing he could do to help his cousin. As Mrs. Wheeler knocked on his sitting room door with a morning tray, he had to compose himself before inviting her to enter.

"Ah, morning Mr. Armstrong," she said, setting down the tray and seeing that her lodger was holding the letter – then nodding towards it. "It came yesterday but you were obviously working late again. Not bad news I hope?"

"Yes, thank you Mrs. Wheeler...er...no...well, it seems everything is bad news these days."

"You're not wrong there sir," said the housekeeper with a resigned sigh as she turned to leave.

Cornelius thanked her for the breakfast tray and sat looking at the modest tea and buttered toast, another reminder of the hard times being experienced by those on the home front as rations became ever more limited. He glanced again at his cousin's letter and reminded himself that others were having it far worse than he.

Mrs Wheeler's daughter Emma had delivered George's letter to Cornelius's rooms an hour before her mother had followed with her lodger's breakfast. The reason the policeman had not received it the previous night was that it was yet another late session that had seen him work into the early hours processing more arrests following yet another night of brawling and disruption in the city.

It had become a cycle of containment, arrest and release – usually without charge – for the authorities, as there were simply too many incidents for the small, local force to deal with. It was a subject Inspector Armstrong was due to discuss with Geoffrey Lyons, the governor of the county gaol that morning. Armstrong's Chief Inspector Henry Baker had been due to meet with Lyons but he had been summoned by the Watch Committee to update them on the latest situation; Baker had therefore asked Armstrong to meet with Lyons on his behalf.

The purpose of the meeting was to establish if there was a better way of dealing with the late-night arrests. The city police force was already stretched to the breaking point -- with leave virtually non-existent for the men, and the cells at the back of the station barely fit for purpose. Governor Lyons had been helping out for over a year by providing temporary cells at the gaol but that in turn, had inevitably increased the pressure on him and his men. Lyons had met with his counterparts from Durham and Lancaster to discuss how they were addressing similar problems, and wanted to share some ideas with his police colleagues.

*

When Inspector Armstrong arrived at the station he was informed by his Desk Sergeant Bill Townsend that he had received a message from the gaol: apparently Governor Lyons was feeling a little under the weather today and he asked if Armstrong could meet him at his house instead. Cornelius therefore spent an hour in his office, taking care of some paperwork before leaving at around ten o'clock.

Geoffrey Lyons and his wife Elspeth lived in one of the beautiful villas at the top of Stanwix Bank – not too far from Chief Constable Henry Baker – that afforded stunning views of the River Eden and Rickerby Park. The morning was made for such a setting and when Cornelius arrived he found Lyons sitting in his garden taking in the moment.

"Good morning Geoffrey, I hear you are not so well?"

The large man levered himself out of a low-sitting deck-chair with some difficulty and stretched out his hand.

"Hello Cornelius," he said, "it's nice to see you. Yes, I think I'm getting too old for this if I'm honest."

Armstrong noted that his normal sallow complexion appeared more ashen than usual; the thick side-whiskers that partly obscured his flaccid jowls were unusually unkempt. He had an air of resignation about him.

Rather than attempt re-entry to the hammock-type chairs, Lyons gestured towards a more conventional table and chairs that stood on a flagged patio in front of large French doors, "Sit yourself down over there Cornelius and I'll organise some refreshment," he said. "Elspeth is getting ready for one of her meetings, but I'm sure she wouldn't mind making us a cup of tea before she goes."

Armstrong was pleased with Geoffrey's suggestion as the thought of trying to conduct a remotely professional conversation in such an awkward position seemed a little comical. He walked over to the patio as Lyons entered the house. On the table was a copy of *The Times;* the policeman picked it up absentmindedly as he waited for his host.

The headline screamed "The Shell Crisis!" The piece went on to re-iterate the shortage of shells available to the troops in France and the need to produce more munitions. David Lloyd George had been appointed as Minister of Munitions to oversee and co-ordinate the production and distribution of munitions for the war effort. One of the initiatives from the ministry was to build a series of munitions factories around the country in order to increase and accelerate the supply to the armies abroad. One site that had been earmarked was Gretna, eight miles north of Carlisle, just over the Scottish border. It was suggested that the factory would consist of four large production sites and two purpose-built townships that would straddle the Scottish/English border.

Armstrong thought of his cousin and understood the need for such a facility but lamented the final lines of the piece that stated that the site would be built by temporary construction workers (a polite term for navvies) who would be shipped in to work on the plant. The policeman had visions of more navvies causing more trouble and exacerbating the already challenging problem that brought him to see Governor Lyons in the first place. As he was contemplating this unenviable thought, his host re-appeared, shortly followed by his wife Elspeth who was carrying a tray on which sat a tea pot and two cups. She was in her outdoor wear, and Armstrong had the impression that she had interrupted her departure to provide some hospitality; not that Elspeth demonstrated anything other than her usual politeness and welcoming demeanour. She had met Armstrong on many a semi-social occasion and was genuinely pleased to see him.

"Good morning, Cornelius," she said as her husband helped with the tray and then added apologetically, "it's lovely to see you but I'm afraid I just have tea to offer, what with the rationing and all."

"Don't worry Elspeth, I understand," said the policeman. "You look lovely if you don't mind me saying."

Mrs. Lyons was a handsome woman who was always immaculately turned out and had a natural grace and dignity about her. She was several years younger than her husband and had an ability to relate to, and converse with, people from all classes with some ease. As she and Cornelius engaged in a brief friendly hug, Elspeth noticed that her guest had spotted another woman standing between the open doors.

"Oh do excuse my rudeness, Cornelius," said Elspeth. She beckoned the considerably younger woman forward, "this is a guest of ours, Miss Katherine Meadows."

"How do you do, Miss Meadows, pleased to meet you," said Armstrong offering a hand.

"How do you do, sir," replied Katherine in a slightly odd accent that the policeman couldn't quite place. She was a slim pretty young woman with a fair complexion and chestnut coloured hair that she wore in the classic pompadour style, on top of which was pinned a wide-brimmed straw cartwheel hat. From under her coat protruded a blue ankle-length skirt. It was almost as though she had styled herself on Elspeth as the older woman was almost identically dressed, save for her wide-brimmed hat being decorated with subtle flowers.

Elspeth continued, "I met Katherine at one of our Suffrage Movement meetings in Manchester. As she told me that she wanted to come up to this area, I invited her to stay, as a sort of lodger if you like," she added turning to Katherine and smiling affectionately.

The young woman appeared embarrassed, "Mrs. Lyons is too kind, Mr. Armstrong. I've found work pretty hard to come by and have been unable to recompense her and Mr. Lyons for their kindness over the past couple of months."

"Nonsense my dear," said Elspeth, "you are more than welcome – you've brought a vitality and enthusiasm to our movement that was lacking before. You are welcome to stay as long as you like."

Katherine smiled her thanks at Elspeth and told Cornelius of her struggles to find regular work in Liverpool, Manchester and now Carlisle. She had spells working at both Hudson Scott's and Carr's Biscuit Factory, but neither position lasted very long. "I found there is discrimination not only against the Irish, Mr. Armstrong, but when you are a woman who voices concerns about equal rights I found I lessened my chances of being accepted still further," she concluded.

"So you are from Ireland originally?" asked the policeman.

Katherine seemed to hesitate before answering, "Yes, I've been in England for over twelve months now. The suffrage movement is more active in England so I was interested in seeing if I could contribute."

"I see. I was unaware you were so active with the Suffragettes Elspeth," said Cornelius turning to the lady of the house.

"I'm not, Cornelius!" replied Mrs. Lyons.

Lyons in mock annoyance. "I am active in the Suffragist Movement but I abhor what the militant faction has done over the past few years. It is *that* group who call themselves Suffra*gettes*. What they don't seem to realise is that their actions are playing directly into the hands of those who oppose women's suffrage, most of whom believe women are silly little creatures who can't be trusted in anything outside the home."

"You're fighting a losing battle here Cornelius," said Lyons with a smile.

"I'm sorry!" said Armstrong defensively, much to the amusement of his hosts. "I'm not defending any sort of discrimination, I long for a society that it based on equality and capability."

"I know you do Cornelius," said Elspeth putting a reassuring hand on his arm, "but sadly there are many men who do not share such a liberal view."

The newspaper was sitting on the table and caught Armstrong's eye; he was reminded of the story of the munitions factory, "I was reading the story about the factory at Gretna earlier – it may provide some employment opportunities?" he said to Miss Meadows, keen to change the subject.

"Yes, I was reading about it myself," said Katherine, "I certainly hope so."

"Anyway," said Elspeth, "I think we should leave these gentlemen to their business."

"Of course," replied her lodger.

The two men stood until the ladies disappeared from view. Resuming their seats, Lyons then apprised Armstrong of his meeting with his opposite numbers from Durham and Lancaster who had worked with their police colleagues to reduce the overcrowding question. Part of their response had apparently been to put pub patrols in place to nip any potential issues in the bud.

"The problem with that," said Armstrong "is that we don't have the manpower to put Bobbies in pubs." He then pointed to the newspaper and made a further point, "and if this factory is built with more navvies, there will be more workers with more disposable income. The problem is in danger of getting worse."

The war comes to Gretna

It seemed as though the world had descended into complete madness by 1915. The First Lord of the Admiralty, Winston Churchill's idea of an offensive in the Near East had failed miserably at some obscure place called Gallipoli; there was even tragedy on the high seas with the loss of the Lusitania. If Sergeant George Armstrong's pre-war prophecy proved accurate during the first half of 1915, then his cousin Cornelius's portent about the further domestic problems caused by the building of the factory at Gretna would prove accurate during the second half of the same year.

But before Inspector Armstrong and his chief constable could contemplate the consequences of the proposed construction, their attention was drawn to the same area on another more pressing matter.

Armstrong was in Henry Baker's office one morning in late May discussing the implications of the Whitehall decision to begin the programme of munitions factories around the country. The two senior policemen were weighing up what it meant for them when there was a knock on the door. Desk Sergeant Bill Townsend partially opened it and leaned in.

"Sorry to disturb you sir but we're getting word of a railway accident near Gretna Green."

Baker, who had been struggling with the problem at hand, was annoyed at the disturbance. He looked up with a furrowed brow at the uniformed officer, "What sort of accident?"

"It's difficult to say at this stage sir, but I've just received a call from the little station up there, and they're wanting some police assistance in the matter." It was clear to Townsend that his superior officer wanted more information so he added as much as he knew. "Apparently it's something about a troop train that may have crashed – it's thought that there might even be one or two deaths."

Baker turned, to Armstrong, "We'll have to come back to this, Cornelius, and deal with the matter at hand. Take a couple of men and get up to Gretna to see what's going on."

"Yes sir." Armstrong was as nonplussed as his chief constable. It was as though he were in a never-ending circle of problem-solving; and once it appeared that he was getting to grips with one, the next one would come out of nowhere and prove to be bigger and more challenging than the last.

That was certainly the case with this latest matter as nothing could prepare him for what he was about to see on that beautiful May morning.

PC Harry Stokes drove the motorised police wagon with Inspector Armstrong in the passenger seat and PC Tommy Gibson perched between the two on a pull-down seat installed in the vehicle just for that purpose. The almost hour-long journey in the rickety vehicle on barely adequate roads began uneventfully; but as the minutes passed and the three policemen got nearer to the site, the feeling of tension mounted as the magnitude of what they were about to encounter began to increase. The vehicle was almost magnetically drawn towards the site, without a word of discussion or a suggestion of direction from any of the three occupants.

Looking out through the open windows as they rattled along, Armstrong and his men first became conscious of an unusual number of people simply standing talking to one another in animated conversation; a little nearer and a further number were running in the direction they were travelling. A little further still and they saw the first plume of smoke a mile or two away; then there was the realisation that the smoke was the result of a fire that still raged below it. Within a few hundred yards of the epicentre of the disaster, the vehicle passed people carrying away blood-soaked victims in the opposite direction, on make-shift stretchers. Cornelius saw that many of the wounded were missing limbs, and he couldn't help but notice they were all soldiers: ragged strands of bloody flesh draping through a soaked khaki uniform. He couldn't help but think of the letter he received from George less than a month earlier, where he described the hell he was witnessing a thousand miles away.

The progressively fearful sights had been matched by the equally terrifying sounds that drew the policemen towards the site: initial silence had given way to audible chatter from people they passed; this in turn had developed into panic-stricken shouting from those who were running to help; and finally there was the ear-piercing shrieking of victims who lay in agony and the wailing of rescuers who wanted to help but didn't know what to do.

Armstrong and his two uniformed men stepped down from their vehicle, barely able to comprehend what they were seeing. A giant engine had been lifted into the air and was straddling an equally large coal wagon that lay sideways across the track. Its carriages had disconnected with the impact and were strewn around the rails at various angles. It was apparent that other trains had also been involved such was the number of engines, carriages and wagons but they were so mangled and plentiful, it was impossible to distinguish which was which and how many trains had actually crashed. It was now around lunchtime but fires still raged from the collisions; Armstrong later learned that it had happened at seven o'clock that morning.

Seemingly hundreds of victims were lying in the surrounding fields in various states of pain and anguish. Some were writhing, screaming and moaning in their death-agony; others just lay still and silent.

Hundreds more were on the scene trying to assist in any way they could, by the time Cornelius and his men arrived. Untrained housewives mixed with qualified medics tending to the victims, while farmers and labourers assisted firemen to tackle the twisted, blazing machinery and act as stretcher bearers. Ominously, intermittent pistol shots could be heard through the smoke and chaos.

Armstrong fought to regain his senses as he was approached by a jacketless young man, whose collarless policeman's shirt and trousers were sodden with sweat and caked in dirt.

"Are you the policemen from Carlisle?" he asked, in his broad accent, "I'm PC Neil Baxter, from Gretna."

"Inspector Cornelius Armstrong," replied the Carlisle man numbly. What on earth happened?" As soon as he asked the question, Armstrong realised the stupidity of it but he couldn't think of anything to say.

"We're not sure whether there were four or even five trains collided this morning sir, around seven o'clock. The two signalmen are to blame – they're over there." Baxter indicated towards the two men who were sitting on the grass about fifty feet away – one was sobbing uncontrollably.

Before approaching them Armstrong issued instructions to his own two constables, "Tommy, you get stuck in here and do what you can to help; Harry you find the nearest telephone and get on to the chief constable telling him that we need as much manpower as we can spare. Also ask him to alert the Cumberland Infirmary as numbers of wounded are going to rise dramatically."

Both men acceded to their superior's orders with a nod and Armstrong accompanied Baxter over to the two signalmen. From what the local policeman told him, coupled with what he could glean from the near-incoherent duo, it seemed the two had an informal arrangement that saw one or the other start work half an hour later than schedule. On this occasion, their own practice had caused confusion between the two as to who had signalled what, with each of the approaching trains. Their confusion had catastrophic consequences with north and southbound trains carrying troops, holiday makers and coals smashing into each other on an unimaginable scale.

As Armstrong gradually came to terms with the magnitude of the disaster, his role throughout the day developed into one of coordinating the constant stream of people turning up to help; and helping with the psychologically demanding task of prioritising the injured personnel who could then be transported to hospitals at Dumfries and Carlisle.

By the end of the day, his appearance resembled that of PC Baxter and everyone else who found themselves involved in the recovery operation: he was caked in sweat and dirt, and his normally piercing blue eyes were lifeless with disbelief. He returned to Carlisle that night with his men – whose number had increased throughout the day – to learn that over two hundred people had been killed in the disaster and it was feared a similar number had been injured.

*

When the Minister of Munitions David Lloyd George decreed the building of factories around the country to increase and accelerate the production of firepower for the troops on the Western Front, he employed the American engineer John Quinin to make the initiative a reality. Quinin looked for remote locations that were far enough away from enemy fire and potential sabotage; yet were close enough to mainline access points in order that materials and weaponry could be quickly transported in and out. The English-Scottish border was perfect in every respect. Every respect that was, in terms of the government's needs. It was anything but perfect as far as the local authorities – and particular the police – were concerned.

The summer and autumn months saw seemingly endless waves of Irish navvies descending on the area to build what was designed as the biggest munitions factory in the country, right on Carlisle's doorstep. The hard-drinking navvies who had caused Inspector Armstrong and his men so much trouble before the war, had more than tripled in number as a they arrived to construct the enormous site that would spread for nine miles across the Dumfries and Galloway border with Cumberland. The four massive production sites would eventually provide work for tens of thousands of people, and with a generation of young men at war, it would be left to the Irishmen and women to staff the factory once it was in operation.

As part of the massive complex, two townships at Eastriggs and Gretna were to be built to house workers; but they would prove to be far too small to accommodate the tens of thousands of migrant workers. Most would find digs in Carlisle which all meant that Armstrong's peace-keeping problems were not likely to end any time soon.

Duty calls

The idea of the munitions factory within a few miles of Carlisle may have caused Inspector Armstrong many a headache regarding the controlling of the social habits of its many workers, but even he could not deny that the construction and commissioning of the facility was an incredible feat. It was completed within thirteen months of the decision being taken in Whitehall to build the factory in the first place. Once the factory was opened, production began immediately and by August 1916 the first cordite was produced and transported to shell factories elsewhere in the country, prior to being shipped across the Channel to France.

The whole enormous complex consisted of four massive production sites and two townships; it had a marshalling yard with rolling stock and its own transport network; there were countless storage sheds; and it had its own power source and water supply system. With so many young men from the British mainland fighting abroad, the majority of the 30,000-strong workforce was comprised of young women, with older men and Irish migrant workers making up a large minority.

One of the workers who had been delighted to secure a position there was Katherine Meadows, Elspeth Lyons's friend and lodger whom Cornelius had initially met the previous year. He was reminded of their introduction when he was re-introduced to her at an afternoon garden party given by his chief constable in the late summer of 1916.

140

Henry Baker and his wife Mary were renowned for their "get-togethers" as they termed them; it seemed Christmas, Easter, summer, in fact any reason would do to host an event for friends and acquaintances. Cornelius was not a great socialite at the best of times and the thought of going through the motions with people he had little in common with during this period of great stress and tension, was only marginally more appealing than the task of arresting endless drunks on the streets after dark. However, he understood Henry's reason for it: it was designed as a little morale-boosting interlude for as many people as he could entertain in his large villa overlooking the River Eden.

This particular gathering was also timed to acknowledge the first shipments of cordite from the factory that – as Henry voiced in his inevitable speech – "…will hopefully help our boys in France and see them victorious!" The equally inevitable cheer went up from those present before everyone slipped into their various desultory party-conversations.

The manager of His Majesty's Munitions Factory Gretna was Kenneth Plummer, who had been personally recommended to Lloyd George by a cabinet colleague, aware of Plummer's twenty-year career as a senior figure at the Woolwich Arsenal. As Plummer was not a local man, Henry Baker had made the effort to introduce himself and as such, had invited him to his afternoon get-together as a courtesy and in an effort to introduce him to other local officials he might find himself dealing with over the coming year or so.

Baker acted almost as chaperone as poor Plummer took in members of the Watch Committee, local councillors and just about anyone else Henry could lay an eye on. At one point he spotted Cornelius who was standing facing the other way listening to Reverend Hope of St. Cuthbert's chatting about the weather and current level of rationing. Armstrong was saved the excruciating experience by his superior's voice from behind and a hand on his shoulder.

"Cornelius, let me introduce you to Mr. Kenneth Plummer, the manager of HM Munitions Gretna." He apologised to Reverend Hope for interrupting; the clergyman smiled understandably and seemed more than happy to turn to the next person and chat to them, probably about the weather and the current level of rationing. Baker turned back to Plummer, "Inspector Cornelius Armstrong is the finest man I have in the city police force."

"How do you do," said Armstrong shaking the man's hand.

Plummer was a small man with a perfectly round, bald head, nattily dressed in a three piece, crisply tailored suit, a high-coloured striped shirt and a yellow spotted bow tie. "Pleased to meet you," he said, "I'm given to understand my workforce causes your workforce a fair amount of problems during their leisure time?"

"You could say that," replied Armstrong trying his best to muster a smile.

The three men chatted for a while before Henry decided it was time to introduce one of his primary guests to someone else. Plummer and Armstrong shook hands once more and the factory manager added, "Let's hope we don't have to meet in our professional capacities Inspector."

"Let's hope so," agreed Cornelius.

As the two men left Armstrong's immediate company, it was at that point that he turned and almost bumped into Elspeth Lyons and her young friend whose name Armstrong initially struggled to remember. "Cornelius, how lovely to see you," said Elspeth, "You remember Katherine?"

"Yes, of course" – and then after a split second – "Katherine Meadows, how nice to see you again."

Just then Elspeth saw her husband Geoffrey beckoning her from across the lawn. "Do excuse me both," she said, "it would appear I'm being summoned!"

"So, how is life treating you Katherine?" Cornelius asked the young woman as Elspeth left them.

"Not too bad sir." She seemed uncomfortable to be alone in the presence of Cornelius, despite the scores of other people milling around them. He put it down to the fact that it was difficult enough for anyone to make garden-party-small-talk, let alone a young woman with an older man she barely knew.

"Forgive me for asking, but have you been ill recently?" asked Armstrong.

She saw that he was looking at her hands that had a yellowish tinge to them, and explained with a smile, "No sir, I managed to secure a position at the factory. One of the jobs they give you is to fill massive basins with acid and cotton; we then wash the mixture in scolding hot water before adding the nitro-glycerine; it's then turned into cordite and packed into bags for transportation. The whole process leaves your skin looking a bit yellow, which is proving very difficult to clean off. One of the men there christened us 'the canary girls' as we're starting to change colour!"

Wondering whether he should bring up the subject of the weather or the current level of rationing, Cornelius instead decided to bring up the subject of Katherine's domestic position, "Are you still lodging with Elspeth?"

"Yes," replied Miss Meadows, "well, rather I should say I am back with her and her husband – they've kindly taken me in again."

She explained that she had left Carlisle not long after the two had met after getting a job at another munitions factory in Manchester.

"That wasn't the one where there was the big explosion was it?" asked Armstrong, remembering something that he read in the newspaper some months ago.

"Yes," said Miss Meadows, "the factory was situated in a built up area and a lot of local residents also died when the thing went up.

"Poor souls," mused the detective, "at least that's not the case at Gretna."

"No it's pretty remote all things considered," said Katherine with a smile.

Armstrong changed the subject, "Tell me Miss Meadows, are you still involved in the suffrage movement?"

Katherine looked puzzled for a couple of seconds before recalling their meeting the previous year when the subject came up. "Oh, yes," and then added after some further thought, "but the movement has quietened down because of the war. It's not without irony Inspector that in a way, women have gained a level of equality as we are now doing men's work while they are away – not that we're getting paid for it mind you. It seems that equality is fine when it suits."

The last comment was barbed but one that Cornelius could not disagree with. He was saved from having to engage further in the subject by Elspeth Lyons who returned to the two after speaking with her husband. He wasn't sure if he or Katherine was the more relieved.

"Honestly," said Elspeth as she approached, "for such an intelligent man he spends an inordinate amount of time flapping about the most trivial things."

The three looked over the heads of the crowd in the direction of Geoffrey who somehow knew he was the subject of his wife's conversation from across the lawn.

"So how are you two getting along?" asked Elspeth.

"Fine," said Cornelius, "Miss Meadows was just telling me about her sojourn to Manchester."

"Yes, it's lovely to have her back," said Elspeth, touching the arm of the young woman affectionately.

The three chatted for a while longer and the afternoon gradually wore on until a number of guests felt they had stayed sufficiently long to make a polite departure. Believing that his duty was done for the afternoon, Cornelius Armstrong took his lead from them and decided to make his excuses.

He first sought out his superior officer whose handshake and expression informed Armstrong that he was aware of his discomfort but appreciated his attendance anyway. As he was leaving, Cornelius then saw Mrs. Lyons again with her young friend. "Elspeth, it was lovely to see you again."

The two hugged. "You too Cornelius, take care."

The policeman turned to Katherine with a more formal offer of his hand, "And to you Miss Meadows, I hope we meet again soon."

The State Management Scheme

If the previous year had not been bad enough, 1916 was probably the hardest year of Inspector Armstrong's career. Like everyone at home, he was burdened by the psychological strain of worry for those fighting abroad. Unlike most however – and instead of the relatively quiet, if vigilant life endured by provincial policemen in Britain – professionally, he faced unrest and disruption on a hitherto unimaginable scale.

Conscription may have been introduced for young single men in January but Irish nationals were exempt; and when the compulsory enlistment was extended to married men a few months later, resentment began to increase amongst the local populace. By mid-summer, as the unbelievable news of the slaughter of the Somme filtered back home, tensions reached breaking point with Inspector Armstrong and his men threatening to be completely overwhelmed by the level of drunkenness and resultant violence that went on involving men and women, on a nightly basis throughout the city.

Armstrong asked Chief Constable Henry Baker if it were possible to draft extra Bobbies in from elsewhere, but Baker's subsequent request to a higher authority was met with a lukewarm response. Instead it was left to the local authorities to recruit special officers to help with police matters, although with the fit young able men conscripted into the army, those who were recruited were limited in their assistance.

"We are spending too much time supervising the special constables," complained Armstrong to his superior a month after their introduction, "and not enough time trying to control the drunkenness."

Unknown to the two policemen, what Baker's representation had done was not only highlight the problem of drunkenness in Carlisle, but to emphasis the detrimental effect such behaviour was having on the production of munitions at the Gretna factory. Sitting in his rooms one night with a pipe and a glass of rum, Cornelius had worked out that the number of arrests made, had increased from a hundred in 1915 to almost a thousand a year later. Baker made it known that if workers were locked up in gaol, they were not contributing to the war effort; and as for those that were in the workplace, what were their productivity levels like when the likelihood was that they would be hungover from the previous night?

An exasperated chief constable made a further appeal to the Watch Committee and the city's corporation, and this time was joined by the magistrates who couldn't keep up with endless cases of factory workers' drunkenness that were brought before them. The chief constable's concerns had not resulted in more men, but his message did finally get through to London, prompting the now-Secretary of State for War, Lloyd George, to repeat his assertion that, "Drink is doing us more damage than all the German submarines put together."

It was finally agreed that the government's central control board would set up a local committee for Carlisle and Gretna to regulate the selling and consumption of alcohol. A meeting was held in the town hall to inform the publicans of the changes that were being implemented. Around fifty chuntering, harrumphing landlords who, like everyone, were suspicious of change crammed into the council chamber.

Before anyone from the board had time to speak, Ernie Jeffers from *The Joiners' Arms* in Caldewgate, spoke above the rumbling crowd, "Although we don't like having glasses smashed and chairs broken, we don't like the thought of having our takings reduced either."

There was a collective chorus of agreement and Brian Kyle from *The Golliah* in Wapping added, "And what about the breweries, how will it affect them?" The question generated more approval from the floor.

"Gentlemen, gentlemen, *please!*" The chairman of the newly formed committee, Alec Cummings, patted the air in front of him in an attempt to gain some order, "All of your questions will be answered, but if we could just have a little bit of order, please."

His words seemed to placate the landlords who took their seats and prepared to listen to what the proposals were. The first thing they were told is that they weren't proposals at all: this was to be a state management scheme that was to be implemented by the government for the benefit and safety of the citizens. Moreover, it was seen as a contribution to the war effort as the current situation was having a detrimental effect on the factory production in Gretna. Cummings added that the government was coming under intense pressure from the temperance movement and had considered other measures such as prohibition, but this experimental scheme had been originally pioneered in Gothenburg, Sweden, and had proved highly successful. It was therefore felt that Britain should have its own experiment and because of the particular problems being experienced in Carlisle, *it* had been identified as the ideal testing ground.

It wasn't a popular message but none of publicans could argue with the premise. The plan was to reduce the amount of drunkenness and disorder in the city by cutting the opening hours of the pubs; having fixed prices; banning special offers; doing away with advertising; and banning the buying of rounds. The scheme would see the government controlling the production and consumption of alcohol by compulsorily purchasing the pubs, as well as the four breweries in the city.

As Cummings read the list out, the audible mumblings from the floor became louder; that was until he came to the last item, "And finally, you will all effectively become government workers and be paid a regular salary. So it will make no difference whether you sell one drink or one hundred drinks during an evening – you and your staff will all be paid a regular wage regardless. "

There was instant silence among the group before Brian Kyle ventured, "That seems all right." One by one, the publicans turned to one another, nodding and mumbling their approval. "How long will this *experiment* last?" asked Kyle.

"We anticipate the scheme lasting for the duration of the war and twelve months thereafter," replied Cummings. "There will be a phased introduction of the scheme that will start immediately."

*

Chief Constable Baker and Inspector Armstrong may well have breathed a collective sigh of relief at the news, but if they thought their troubles were over they were to be mistaken, as the implementation of the scheme caused confusion and disruption that for a period matched the disorderly behaviour that had prompted the changes in the first place. One of the worst incidents took place at the Iredale Brewery on Currock Street in Wapping.

It was a late autumn morning when Armstrong was called out and led a group of fifteen uniformed officers over the Victoria Viaduct and down James Street into Wapping. What greeted them was a crowd of two- to three-hundred people, jostling one another and shouting obscenities at the building, presumably aimed at the officials inside who were working on the closure of the building. Their aim was to consolidate the four breweries in the city into one, state owned facility in Caldewgate.

Like Caldewgate and Shaddongate, Wapping was a rundown area that was home to hundreds of families and, latterly, to a similar number of Irish migrant munition workers. Chimneys belched black smoke over rows of tenements. Behind the dwellings, shared privies gave off an appalling odour that was scented by the stink of malt and hops from the brewery – residents were oblivious to the smell. The pawnbrokers on Water Street did a roaring trade each Monday as women took anything of value to exchange for cash that would last them until pay day on Friday.

In the absence of their husbands, many of the women worked in the brewery and at Hudson Scott's tin box factory at the top of James Street. They saw the closure of

Iredale's as yet another exploitation of the working classes. If female workers thought they were being discriminated against before the war, they were more vulnerable than ever to being taken advantage of during it. They made up a large number of the crowd protesting against the scheme. Numbers were swelled by scores of Irishmen, who had gone along for the *craic* – and if there was a bit of trouble to be caused, well, that was all the better. Among the Irish contingent were Sean O'Doyle and Michael McGinty.

The shrill of a policeman's whistle prompted heads to turn in the crowds, prompting the noise level to rise and the jostling to intensify. As if triggered by the whistle, a brick hurled from somewhere near the back of the crowd sailed through the tobacco-filled air and smashed through one of the first floor windows of the brewery, generating a loud cheer from the mob. Realising it was futile to try and single out individuals out for arrest, Armstrong concentrated his men on simply breaking up the crowd.

"He seems to know what he's doing!" O'Doyle shouted above the din of the crowd to McGinty and pointed across to the policeman in the Homburg and knee-length overcoat. *"He'll spoil all our fun!"* The smile suddenly dropped from his face when he spotted another face in the crowd; in truth it wasn't so much the face as the stature of the man that caught O'Doyle's eye.

McGinty saw the change in his friend's demeanour and followed his gaze across the rowdy sea of faces to where he was staring. He too looked incredulously at the man who towered above everyone else. "Isn't that O'Connell?" he asked Sean.

"I do believe it is Michael my boy!" replied his friend, "and you know what that means!"

Like many of his countrymen Seamus O'Connell was a navvy who travelled to the mainland looking for work and ended up like so many others, securing a job at the munitions factory. That wasn't the reason O'Doyle was interested in him however. O'Connell's reputation for being the best bare-knuckle fighter in Belfast had spread far and wide from his home city, to the extent that he was now considered the best exponent of the brutal pastime throughout the whole of Ireland. His arrival in Carlisle was destined to set in motion a series of events that would lead to a tragic outcome which no one could have predicted.

The fight

"So, whad'ya think Michael?"

O'Doyle and McGinty had returned to their digs following the police successfully breaking up the morning's excitement. Like all rented tenements, theirs was a drab, colourless dwelling with limited facilities. The one luxury it afforded was a second bedroom, which gave each man a little privacy. Across the stone landing lived Vi Smith and her five children, all crammed into a one-bedroom flat. Vi's husband – like virtually all men of his age – was away fighting on the Western Front. Despite the various nefarious activities the two Irishmen engaged in, in a show of human kindness, they often made sure Vi had extra bread or milk for the children. Word of their altruism naturally spread throughout the whole block and the two were well thought of as a result.

"I don't know," said McGinty pouring himself a cup of tea and returning to his wooden chair on the opposite side of the fire to Sean. "Do we need the money? We've got a good thing going here."

"You're not scared are you?" As soon as O'Doyle uttered the words he regretted it, as he saw McGinty's face flash with rage. "I'm sorry Michael," he said quickly, getting out of his seat and putting his hand on his friend's shoulder, "that was uncalled for; you're the bravest man I know. I was only joking."

"It's just with this new state management carry-on it might not be as easy to sort out."

Since being in England, the two had organised three bare-knuckle contests, one taking place at *The Golliah Inn* close to where they were staying in Carlisle. McGinty was well-known in Ulster as being one of the best exponents of the sport and his name alone had drawn crowds of his fellow countrymen to the contest, making him and O'Doyle – regardless of the result – a lot of money into the bargain. For the record, McGinty had won all of his bouts fairly convincingly.

McGinty may have been *one* of the best known fighters among his kind, but Seamus O'Connell was renowned as being at the very top of the illegal pastime. His supporters – of which there were many – claimed he could give Jack Johnson a run for his money. He was also undefeated after a couple of dozen fights but the one that evaded both men was the one that pitted each one against each other. There had been talk of setting up a contest in Belfast a couple of years earlier but it never came to anything as McGinty and O'Doyle had to get out of Ireland quickly. Now, bizarrely, the two best fighters in Ireland had an opportunity to meet in a back street in Carlisle of all places.

"You're a competitor Michael, a fighter," said Sean, "surely that appeals to ye? Just think, this could be your last fight and what a way to go, beating *King O'Connell* and finishing your career undefeated!"

McGinty broke into a half smile, attracted by the thought but still with reservations about the risks. "It's all right for you Sean. You've got Kathleen" – a reference to O'Doyle's girlfriend – "and it's not you who's in the ring."

"C'mon Michael, this could be a big pay day for us both. At least let me make a few enquiries; I didn't see

O'Donnell's handler, Lynch, in the crowd but I'm sure he won't be far away. Let me hunt him out and see if we can get something organised."

It wasn't McGinty's pocket that was tempted, it was his ego; he knew by beating the mighty O'Connell he would not only remain undefeated he would achieve notoriety throughout the whole of Ireland. "Okay Sean," he said after some thought, "see what you can do and we'll take it from there."

*

Although like Sean and Michael, Mick Lynch and Seamus O'Connell were staying in Carlisle and working at the munitions factory in Gretna, their paths hadn't crossed; the two Antrim men stayed in Wapping, the two Belfast men had digs in Caldewgate, and both pairs worked in different areas of the factory.

With the increase in migrant workers to the city however, Carlisle was becoming a mini-Ireland where everyone was getting to know everyone else, and it wasn't long before O'Doyle made contact with O'Connell's handler through an intermediary. Unlike Sean, O'Connell and Lynch hadn't spotted their two Antrim counterparts amongst the mob outside Iredale's, so when Lynch heard of their presence in Carlisle, his eyes lit up as O'Doyle's had, at the excited thought of his man meeting the best opponent possible. The thought of the amount of money that could be made from such a fight excited him more.

Their territorial roots had followed them across the Irish Sea and there was a reluctance to meet in either Caldewgate or Wapping, as it was considered the other's patch – the fact that neither man hailed from Carlisle or even knew the city particularly well had little to do with their respective reservations. It was agreed therefore that O'Doyle and Lynch would meet at *The Old Black Bull Inn* on Annettwell Street near the castle – neutral ground.

The two had never actually met but knew each other by sight. O'Doyle arrived and scoured the raucous pub until he spotted Lynch through the smoke and the crowd; he was sitting in the far corner leaning on a trestle table – not exactly quiet but as good as it was going to get for the clandestine meeting.

"Michael Lynch, I presume?" said O'Doyle, after appearing at Lynch's side through the crowd.

"Sean O'Doyle, I presume?" countered the Belfast man.

The two grudgingly shook hands and O'Doyle sat down to discuss the possibility of their respective friends meeting in the ring. It was quickly established that both parties were receptive to the idea, knowing the income such a bout would generate among the Irish population. The problem was finding an appropriate venue to hold such a big event that would be large enough to hold the number that would want to attend, and yet be discreet enough to remain out of the prying eyes of the authorities, especially with the recent introduction of the state management scheme.

"I think I know the place," said Sean, "I think Brian Kyle at the *Golliah* would let us hold it."

"That's on your home turf!" protested Lynch.

"Cut yerself on Mick, we're not in the homeland now! He has a large stable at the back of the pub where we've organised a fight before. It's big enough to get a couple of hundred people in and if I know Brian, I think he'll be okay with the suggestion. Let me arrange a meeting between the three of us and we'll take it from there."

Lynch agreed to the common-sense approach suggested by O'Doyle, who spoke to the landlord of the *Golliah* the following night.

"I don't know Sean, since they introduced State Management, we're watched closely and inspected regularly." The publican was clearly in a quandary; the proposed event may well be illegal but it would certainly make him a lot of money. Before O'Doyle could employ any further powers of persuasion, Kyle continued, almost to himself, "Mind you if I invited the control board inspector the night before and convinced him everything was going okay, and then arranged it for a Sunday night when it's quieter, we should be able to get away with it."

"Good lad Brian!" Sean had to consciously stop himself from raising his voice, such was his satisfaction. He thanked the landlord and rushed away to tell Michael and get a message to the opposition.

*

In the subsequent weeks, news spread of the impending contest among the thousands of Irishman in the area. The two biggest bare-knuckle fighters in Ireland could have filled Phoenix Park, Dublin, but here they were, about to meet in a converted stable at the back of a pub in Carlisle. Not that that diminished the excitement among those who knew the significance of the bout.

As planned, Brian Kyle invited the unsuspecting board inspector round to the *Golliah* on the Saturday before the fight, and allowed him to go through his books and check that everything was in order. The pub itself was a shabby looking establishment; upon being built some years earlier it had been coated in a white render that was now blackened, through a combination of age and soot from the surrounding area. Inside was much like any similar establishment: stone floors covered with a light dusting of sawdust, on which stood wooden benches and trestle tables. But it was the rear of the building that set it aside from most other pubs. What was once a stable had been converted into a room that could be used for anything from storing sacks and barrels, to holding illegal fights, regardless of whether the protagonists were human or animal.

Twenty-four hours after the board inspector had signed the pub off as having passed its intermittent review, the back room was ready for the biggest event of its kind seen in the north of England. It was packed with onlookers who had arrived early to ensure they secured a place.

Walking into the room was an assault on the senses. The first thing that hit the entrant was the almost intolerable stench: a comingled stink of sweat, beer and tobacco smoke created a heavy atmosphere that caused eyes to sting and made breathing a conscious chore. The toxic air was exacerbated by the almost deafening noise emitted by the hundreds of Irishmen, and as many middle-aged locals who had managed to get in, fully aware of the significance of the contest.

The room was virtually black save for a circular ring in the centre about fifteen paces in diameter that had been created by erecting tall wooden pillars; waist-high boards were fixed to the timber posts over which leaned dozens of snarling, baying faces. Across the top of the ring were draped six cables to which were fixed temporary lighting that illuminated the ring and accentuated the darkness elsewhere in the large room.

Finally at ten o'clock the two men entered the room to be greeted by a frenzied, ear-splitting roar. Books were being run at various areas of the room and as the spectators saw the two fighters, there was a renewed scramble to bet on the outcome.

Both McGinty and O'Connell were stripped to the waist; two of the boards on opposite sides of the ring were removed to allow them to enter. Sweat and grime glistened on their heads and torsos as the temporary lighting swung overhead. O'Connell was an enormous man – if anything, bigger than McGinty – with a history of violent convictions behind him. Those who had the misfortune to get close to him invariably concluded that it wasn't so much that he was incredibly brave and fearless, but simply unbalanced and dangerous.

Sean O'Doyle stood on the other side of the board behind his friend Michael – no words were necessary. Mick Lynch stood on the opposite side and took the lead as a kind of master-of-ceremonies.

"All right!" he shouted, not standing a chance of being heard against the din. "We know what we are here for! The winner will be declared when one of them can't carry on!"

All the while, O'Connell and McGinty just stared at one another, expressionless. If it were possible, the bout was made all the more significant due to the sectarian nature of the two men: McGinty was known to be a staunch Unionist while O'Connell was a fierce Nationalist. Both sides of the religious and political divide were represented and that gave an angry edge to those outside the ring as well as those inside. An even louder roar went up when the two men were signalled to start.

O'Connell was the first to connect with a meaningful blow to McGinty's jaw; the jab was swift and precise, something that surprised many onlookers who had never seen the apparently big, lumbering giant fight before. It threw McGinty back towards the edge of the ring and prompted a raucous cheer from the supporters of the Belfast man. McGinty quickly shook off the setback however and stooping low, came up with a left-right combination that rocked O'Connell – an equally piercing cheer came from his supporters.

O'Connell then tried to repeat the jab that had brought success moments earlier but McGinty blocked with his forearm and in the same movement hammered a fist against the side of his opponent's cheek – it made a cracking sound that only the two combatants heard amid the racket. The bigger man winced with pain but almost as quickly shook off the discomfort and reset himself. This time it was McGinty who swung and missed which allowed O'Connell a free left hand to the ribs; he didn't miss and there was another sound of breaking bones.

On it went for ten minutes or more, with both men throwing punches that would have easily incapacitated any ordinary man. As the giants began to show signs of tiredness, O'Connell lurched forward trying to land a haymaker, only for McGinty to dodge the oncoming missile and counter with a punch to the diaphragm that again caused the big man wince and this time, fall to one knee.

The noise was deafening by this point; both men were bleeding heavily and every punch that connected fuelled the barbaric, saliva-spraying supporters who took it in turns to raise their bottles and wave their make-shift betting papers in the air every time their man landed a punch on his opponent.

From his semi-kneeling position O'Connell drove upwards and lifted McGinty off his feet sending him backwards into one of the boards; he took the full force of the collision in the small of his back, something that knocked the wind out of him. The two broke into a wrestling contest as arms and legs flayed almost as one eight-limbed beast. As McGinty tried to force himself and his opponent off the boards and back into the centre of the ring, in the grappling mayhem he lost balance and fell to the floor with the full weight of his opponent on top of him. Whatever air was left in his lungs from the collision with the board was driven out of him with a squeal that prompted another cacophonous roar from the O'Connell supporters.

Any similarity the illegal sport had to organised boxing under Queensbury Rules disappeared completely at this point, when it descended into a show of gratuitous violence that was about to sicken all those present.

With his opponent virtually incapacitated underneath him O'Connell leaned his head down and bit off the fleshy lobe of McGinty's ear. The Antrim man cried out and instinctively reached toward his injury with both hands. This left him completely defenceless to O'Connell who scrambled from his knees to his feet and hurled his twenty-stone frame down, smashing his elbow into McGinty's unprotected face, shattering his teeth and smearing his nose across his face. The uncontrolled cheering throughout the former stable instantly morphed into a disbelieving gasp, as the spectators couldn't quite believe what they had just witnessed.

O'Connell was undeterred and unrepentant, as he followed up his barbaric action with a series of right-left blows to the, now unconscious, man's head.

"That's enough Seamus!" shouted Mick Lynch to his man, who didn't appear to hear. Lynch and Sean O'Doyle simultaneously vaulted the barriers to stop the madman. Others joined and between them, they managed to pull O'Connell off and drag him to the side. He sat with his back against one of the perimeter boards, staring into the middle distance. He was bleeding heavily from the nose and mouth, and had sustained a fractured cheek bone and several broken ribs. Not surprisingly however, he came off the better of the two.

McGinty lay motionless amid the sawdust that was now a congealed sludge created by sweat and blood. Sean looked down in desperation at his friend who was virtually unrecognizable from the man who had entered the pub earlier in the evening. His cheekbones were misshapen and his eye sockets, splintered to the point of being able to see fragments of white bone through the bloody mess. McGinty moaned lightly giving his friend some encouragement – as he had vaulted the barrier he honestly believed Michael was dead. The only other sound was someone vomiting in the darkness after having witnessed the atrocity.

Finally, a local's voice came from behind, "We've got a cart outside, let's get him up to the infirmary."

A group of men lifted and dragged the dead weight of a man back through the pub and loaded him on to the horse drawn cart. The man who appeared to have organised it, signalled to the driver and said to Sean, "This is Gilly Millholme, he'll get you and your pal up there in double quick time."

Sean O'Doyle clambered on the back of the cart and knelt beside his supine friend. As the rag and bone man slapped his horse into motion, there were several things racing through O'Doyle's head, not least of which was how would he carry out his plans for the following Tuesday now that Michael was unavailable to help him.

Another call from over the Border

Inspector Armstrong was met at the main gate of the factory and taken to the office of Kenneth Plummer, the manager to whom the policeman had been introduced at Henry Baker's garden party a few months earlier. Unsurprisingly on this occasion, Plummer had a very different disposition from the one he demonstrated during their last encounter. He had called Chief Constable Baker earlier that morning after a catastrophic explosion had occurred at the factory during the night. Living close by in Gretna, he was awakened by the loud bang just after two o'clock. Within minutes his phone was ringing with confirmation from one of his night shift managers that there had been a blast in the drying section of the factory, always considered to be the most dangerous section as it was the end of the munitions process. Plummer raced to the scene to discover a corner of the building had been blown out and it was known that there were at least six fatalities. After two hours' assessment by the military police it was decided to involve the civil force as one of the victims could not be identified and the fear was that it was an attempted sabotage.

Plummer took it upon himself to contact the chief constable of the city force in Carlisle, having been acquainted with him since his arrival in the area. When Henry Baker heard of the disaster, he in turn, nominated his best officer to carry out the initial investigation.

"A terrible business, inspector," said Plummer after Cornelius Armstrong had been shown into his office and

165

the customary pleasantries were exchanged. "Less than six months into the production, and we are already faced with this!"

"Try not to distress yourself too much Mr. Plummer," said Armstrong, trying to give the man some comfort. "It was always going to be a hazardous enterprise given the nature of the materials you are handling here."

"I suppose so," said the manager, "but to lose workers in this manner is devastating. Heaven only knows how their families will take it."

"I'm aware that there have been similar occurrences in other munitions factories around the country."

"Yes but they were known to be accidents – occupational hazards if you like. The fear here is that it is attempted sabotage."

"Well first things first," said the inspector, "can we visit the site of the blast?"

"Yes, yes, of course," replied Plummer, shaking himself from his absentmindedness.

Plummer had a driver waiting outside his office and he and the detective were taken a mile or so to one of the further corners of the complex. The location and scale of the incident needed no explanation to the visitor. A large brick building which Plummer informed Cornelius was the drying section had one corner completely collapsed. Chunks of masonry littered the ground. Two objects covered in blood-stained sheets were lying a few yards from what would have been one of the entrances to the building.

"Is it safe to enter?" asked Armstrong getting out of the car.

166

"Yes, I think so," replied the manager, "we have a buildings department and they have surveyed the damaged area. The reason it is not cleared away is simply because I wanted you to see it first."

"Thank you," said Cornelius stepping carefully towards the building. Even with a gaping hole in the structure, the vapours of the explosive materials were still noticeable. He picked his way past what were obviously the first two victims, and entered. The interior was as imposing as the exterior, such was its size. On the ground were another three covered victims at the rear of the one of the large stoves, and what appeared to be a sixth deceased who was positioned nearer to what was once the door. This poor creature had apparently taken the full force of the blast as other smaller sheets were scattered yards away from the larger object, presumably covering various body parts that had been blown from the torso.

Other than the area where the two men stood, the materials and equipment elsewhere within the large building remained largely unaffected.

Inspector Armstrong mumbled to himself, "This is obviously the direction of the explosion." He indicated with his two arms outspread towards the devastated corner of the building.

"Yes," agreed Plummer, "I'm reluctant to use the word *lucky,* but it could have actually been worse had the force of the blast carried inward instead of outward. As it was, it was strong enough to kill these three poor girls as well as the two people outside." He drew the policeman's attention to the sixth victim, "Unlike the others who remained virtually intact, this poor man was literally blown to pieces.

"He was the reason I wanted your involvement inspector as he is the only victim whom we can't identify. He has no identification and the supervisor from the railway shed, where the other male victim was based, didn't recognise him as one of his workers."

Cornelius pulled back the sheet: the man had been almost blown in half. The torso was barely attached to the legs by strands of tendons and bloody innards. A full shoulder and arm were missing on the right side and a forearm and foot were missing from the left. The sickening sight reminded Cornelius of the scene of devastation he had witnessed a few miles away at Quintishill eighteen months earlier. He walked over to one of the other smaller sheets that lay several yards away. It was the man's arm from the elbow down.

He studied the hand; the fingertips were a distinctive shade of saffron – the tell-tail sign of a heavy smoker – but the rest of the hand also had a yellowish hue. "Are you sure this man didn't work here, Mr. Plummer?" he asked, removing yet another sheet to reveal the man's other arm. "His hands have that yellow colour like many of your other workers."

"I never picked up on that inspector," said Plummer, "I'll certainly double-check but there don't appear to be any other workers unaccounted for."

Armstrong inspected the other three bodies within the building and shook his head sadly, "What a damn shame," he said under his breath, "what a waste."

"Two of them were sisters," added Plummer, "Morag and Isla Stewart who apparently just lived down the road with their mother. The third young woman is Amy Flowers, a married woman from Dumfries."

The policeman read the manager's thoughts: *As if the situation couldn't be any worse.*

Armstrong went back over to the unidentified man and carefully lifted his jacket to try his inside pockets. All he came up with was a tin containing a few rolled up cigarettes and a book of matches on which was the legend *The Ship Inn, Gatehouse of Fleet.* "Are workers allowed matches and cigarettes on site?" he asked.

"No," replied Plummer, "they have all been briefed on the perils of carrying them but in reality it is extremely difficult to control given the vast workforce."

"Gatehouse of Fleet," said Armstrong, "that's quite a distance from here isn't it?"

"I'm not sure," said Plummer, who was not from the area. "The obvious point is that people do travel from all around the area to work here." He then reviewed his own comment, "But then again this man doesn't appear to have worked here at all."

Armstrong slipped the book of matches into his own pocket, "If this man wasn't familiar with the factory, I suppose the cigarettes and matches could have been the cause of the explosion.

"Who are the two outside?" he asked.

"One was an Irish chap who worked in the railway shed opposite." Plummer pointed to the adjacent building that appeared unscathed other than the bizarre sight of a motorised van wedged up against it after apparently having been blown onto its side as a result of the blast. "The van belonged to the young man," added Plummer following Armstrong's gaze.

The two walked over to the two remaining bodies and Plummer drew back the sheet from the man. As he did so Armstrong's attention was taken by three green army vehicles with red crosses that were approaching. "This was Sean O'Doyle," said Plummer above the noise created by the vehicle engines, "he was one of the navvies who helped build the factory and then stayed on to work here. I believe he lived in Carlisle."

Armstrong looked back down after momentarily being distracted by the ambulances, just as Plummer dropped the sheet back down over the man he identified as O'Doyle. The policeman didn't properly see the deceased therefore but didn't think too much of it as he reached to uncover the final body. "And this?" he said revealing the final victim. "*My God!*" he cried before Plummer could answer.

"You know this woman? Is she a friend of yours?"

"Yes, well a friend *of* a friend you could say," replied Armstrong, searching for her name.

"Her name is Katherine Meadows," said Plummer.

"Of course, Katherine Meadows," repeated Armstrong. "She is a friend and lodger of an acquaintance of mine in Carlisle. I was talking to her at that garden party when you and I first met in August."

"Oh yes, the one at Chief Constable Baker's home," recalled Plummer.

"Yes, Miss Meadows lodged with neighbours of the Bakers. Elspeth will be devastated when she hears the news."

"Can we remove the bodies?" asked one of the drivers climbing out of his army ambulance.

"Yes, I think I've seen enough," said Armstrong. Then turning back to the manager of the factory, "You were right to contact us Mr. Plummer – we need to identify the other victim and establish whether or not he had any connection with any of the other victims. Perhaps more importantly, we need to find out if this was an accident or a deliberate attempt to sabotage the plant and if so, what is the likelihood of further attempts."

Aftermath

That afternoon Armstrong visited the Lyons's villa to inform them of the tragedy. He was shown in by Mary, the wife of his Chief Constable Henry. Given the closeness, both in terms of proximity and personal relationship the Bakers and Lyons shared, it was natural that she felt the need to spend some time giving comfort to Elspeth. The fact that she was here at all told Armstrong that the Lyons had already heard the news.

"They are in the sitting room Cornelius," she said indicating. She then reached for her coat and informed the inspector she felt it more appropriate that she leave at this point, "They are upset enough without too many people hovering about."

Armstrong thanked Mary and went into the sitting room where he found Geoffrey Lyons consoling his wife who was in floods of tears. The room was decorated in preparation for Christmas, but the tree and ornaments looked completely inappropriate, given the current circumstance.

"I'm so sorry, Elspeth," he said, "I know Katherine was a dear friend."

He exchanged helpless glances with Lyons as Mrs. Lyons fought to compose herself. Finally she raised her head from her lap and blew her nose for the umpteenth time, something she would have ordinarily been mortified at doing under normal circumstances. Her husband peeled a fresh handkerchief from a small pile that sat beside him on the settee and gave it to his wife, allowing her to wipe her bloodshot eyes.

"I just can't believe such a lovely young woman could be taken in this way," she said to no one in particular.

Geoffrey asked "Do we know how it happened, Cornelius?"

"Well," started the policeman taking a seat opposite the couple, "sadly Katherine was one of six people killed in the blast. Somehow a fire seems to have started in the drying section of the factory where Katherine was working. This in turn appears to have ignited the crude explosives, causing a massive explosion."

"A tragic accident then," concluded Lyons.

"Probably," said Armstrong, "although there are one or two issues that I am looking into. In particular, one of the deceased hasn't yet been identified."

"How awful," said Mrs. Lyons, having regained some composure. "I remember Katherine telling me she wasn't looking forward to the week ahead as she was working in the drying area which was apparently her least favourite job of all."

"Yes I believe she was one of a group who carried out different tasks on a six weekly rota," said Armstrong, "Fate had it that she was doing that duty at that place at that time."

"How awful," repeated Mrs. Lyons, then referring to the unidentified victim she added, "There must be hundreds of families around the area worried sick about a loved one who works at the factory."

"That's the strange thing Elspeth, no one has come forward reporting a loved one missing. It's possible that the person lived alone but it seems that all of the other victims – and all of the other workers on site for that matter – were all accounted for."

"There must be some sort of clocking-in system I assume?" asked Geoffrey.

"Yes that's right," confirmed Armstrong, "Katherine was one of four women who were tragically killed in the blast – they were all identified by the clocking-in system and the fact that everyone was present at the roll call that followed. Similarly with one of the men who was killed, but there was a second man who has yet to be identified. No one else is missing from the staffing lists and no one can throw any light on a visitor who may have been there."

"And why would a visitor be in that area of the factory?" asked Lyons rhetorically.

"Precisely," agreed the inspector. "One possibility could be that this man was there without authorisation and with nefarious intentions to sabotage the plant."

"How terrible!" exclaimed Mrs. Lyons, "surely no one would be so cruel?"

"There are some wicked people in this world my dear," said Geoffrey, again putting his arm around his wife.

"I have to look into all possible lines of inquiries I'm afraid," said Armstrong "And on that subject Elspeth, would you mind if I take a look at Katherine's room please, just as a routine part of the investigation?"

"Of course," Elspeth showed the inspector up to the first floor landing, "it's the second door on the right Cornelius," she said indicating, "would you like me to stay?"

"No there is no need, Elspeth." Whilst fully understanding the need to go through someone's personal belongings, it was something Inspector Armstrong hated doing; he himself was proud of the few personal possessions he owned and the thought of someone rooting through them was abhorrent to him. Having to do that to others therefore never ceased to make him feel uncomfortable. Given his discomfort of the task ahead, he felt it best to approach it alone, especially given that Elspeth was particularly close to Katherine and couldn't fail to become further upset in her witnessing of the process. When he explained this to her, he sensed her relief as it was something she clearly didn't want to be involved in either. Elspeth returned downstairs therefore and allowed the policeman to enter her lodger's room alone.

Inside, Armstrong's first impression was that it was neat but modestly presented. The colours of the room were plain and neutral: pale blue walls – on which there were no pictures – that complemented a slightly darker shade of carpet and a simple white bed spread. The only two items to break up the plainness of the room were a small, oval, multi coloured rug that lay at the foot of the bed, incongruous with its surroundings; and a large walnut unit consisting of two wardrobes that were connected either side by a central dresser that had three draws and incorporated a mirror. It sat against the wall opposite the window.

Armstrong scanned the somewhat simple room and inevitably gravitated towards the wall unit. Below the mirror was white lace dresser cloth, to the side of which was the only photograph that was to be seen anywhere in the room: it was a portrait of Millicent Fawcett, founder of the National Union of Women's Suffrage.

He opened the top drawer of the dresser. The contents were as modest as the rest of the room: there was a Bible, a telegram and a small jewellery box. Armstrong flicked through the bible to see if there were any inserts – there weren't. He then picked up the telegram which carried the rather cryptic message:

PADRAIG FROM MOSSYARD WILL BE THERE
END
S

The detective mulled over the message for a few minutes before finally opening the jewellery box. It contained two items; the first was a ring that looked a little old fashioned for a young woman. *A mother or grandmother's ring perhaps?* The second item was a pretty heart-shaped locket that hung on the end of a gold chain. Armstrong found the tiny mechanism on one side of the heart and it flipped open in response to the pressure of his thumb nail. Two minute pictures – one of a man, one of a woman – had been delicately inserted into each of the gallery windows of the locket. Squinting at the pictures Cornelius could see that the woman was Katherine herself. There was no indication as to who the man was – *maybe this mysterious Padraig?*

He snapped the locket shut and slipped it in his overcoat pocket along with the telegram before looking through the other drawers and the wardrobes. They contained nothing other than Katherine's clothes so Armstrong returned downstairs to re-join Geoffrey and Elspeth Lyons whom he found sitting in silence, staring blankly out of the window.

Geoffrey was the first to snap out of his reverie as the policeman walked into the room. "Did you find anything of any interest Cornelius?"

Armstrong took the locket and the telegram from his pocket, "Yes there were a couple of interesting items." Referring to the telegram he asked, "Does the name Padraig mean anything to you? There's a reference to him in this telegram."

He handed it first to Geoffrey who shook his head before passing it to his wife. "I've never heard Katherine talk about any young man before," said Elspeth. "Now that you mention it, it is something that never occurred to me in the past."

"The telegram was in the draw of her dresser along with this," said Armstrong producing the locket and chain. He passed it to Elspeth, who looked as puzzled as she had at the content of the telegram.

"What a pretty locket," she said, as she instinctively searched for the opening mechanism, just as Cornelius had done a few minutes earlier. Once it opened in her hands, Elspeth again expressed her surprise, "Well I never! It seems that Katherine has been quite close to this Padraig. It's so strange that she has never mentioned him."

"I found the locket in a small jewellery box in the draw. It also contained a ring that I left in there, but if you have no objections I would like to take the telegram and the locket with me."

"Why would you want to take them Cornelius?" asked Elspeth.

"Oh, it's just routine," said the policeman, "nothing to worry about. I don't suspect Katherine of any wrongdoing, but as there are a few loose ends regarding the investigation, I would like to hold on to them until it is finally sorted out. I promise I'll return them as soon as it's done."

"Thank you Cornelius, although they don't belong to us any more than they belong to you," said Elspeth.

"Perhaps you could re-trace Katherine's steps back to Manchester and her involvement in the Suffrage Movement there my dear," said Geoffrey to his wife, "that way we may be able to find any relatives."

"That's a good idea Geoffrey," agreed Armstrong; it was a line of enquiry he intended to follow himself but was reluctant to discourage Elspeth and it would act as a distraction from the grief that was affecting her so badly.

On his way back to the station, Inspector Armstrong puzzled over the two items that he carried in his pocket. He prided himself in knowing all of the lanes, courts and yards of the city but the one referred to in the telegram was a new one on him. Upon his arrival, he tested the local knowledge of his Desk Sergeant. "Bill, do you know where Moss Yard is?"

Bill Townsend thought for a while before venturing, "I think it's down at the back of London Roa…oh no, hang on… that's Myer's Yard". He gave the matter a little more thought; like Armstrong he was a local man born and bred and it annoyed him that he didn't know the answer. "I'm not sure to be honest sir," he said at last.

"No, neither am I," said his superior.

"I'll make a point of looking into it," said Townsend.

A sinister turn

It was mid-morning the day following Armstrong's visit to Lyons's villa. He was sitting at his desk when he heard a familiar voice talking to Sergeant Townsend through his open door, prompting him to see what was going on at the front desk.

"*Seth?*" he exclaimed from the doorway of his office.

Seth Graham, the carter from Shaddongate was standing in front of the desk giving Bill Townsend some details that the sergeant was writing down. Cornelius was incredulous, never having seen Seth out of his natural environment in all the years he had known him; he looked completely out of place.

"Hello Mr. Armstrong," he said, "I'm just reporting a theft – somebody's nicked one of me transporters."

As Seth was apprising Armstrong of the reason for his extraordinary visit, someone else appeared at the front desk wanting Sergeant Townsend's attention.

"It's all right Bill," said Cornelius, "you see to this gentleman and I'll deal with Seth." He invited Graham into his office, amused that for the first time ever it was he who was hosting the old man and not the other way around. "I've just made a cuppa, can I get you one?"

"Wouldn't say no sir, thank you," said the carter removing his hat revealing a completely bald dome of a head – another first.

Armstrong took the kettle from the top of the stove and poured the hot water through a tea strainer into a tin mug.

"That's lovely sir, thank you very much." Seth wrapped both hands around the mug as if to warm his hands. It was not a particularly cold day but a combination of his poor circulation and his being in an unfamiliar, uncomfortable environment prompted the action. Armstrong sensed the working man's discomfort and sought to put him at his ease. He closed the door and invited him to take a seat.

"Now Seth, what's the story?" Armstrong believed that this supposedly petty crime might provide some light relief from some of the more tasking matters he had to deal with.

"Well," started the carter, "there's been a bloke who has regularly hired the van over the past few months."

"The van?" interrupted the inspector, unaware that Graham had anything other than horse-drawn vehicles.

"Yeah, I got one of them new-fangled vehicles last year. Don't like it mysel' – can't even drive it! Rather have horses any day, but as more and more people was asking about hiring I ended up getting one. It's done me good in fairness – had plenty of work wid it. Anyway this Irish fella cem in the yard a few months back and told me he wanted it every six weeks or so. Everything went like clockwork – every six weeks he would come in, hire the van for a couple of days, pay up front and return it as good as gold. That was until this last time. As I say, he normally hires it for a couple of days, but he's been gone a week now and the bugger hasn't come back. I've been round to the address he give me but there's nobody there. I reckon he's done a flit."

"Where is the address?" asked Armstrong, reaching for a pen and paper.

"He stays in one of the tenements in Wapping – Robert Street."

"What was the bloke's name?"

"O'Doyle."

Armstrong looked up from his notebook. Up until that point he had believed Seth's problem to be a fairly minor issue; one that prompted him to help an old acquaintance in need as much as solving any crime. But now, like a flash of light, the one name uttered by the carter had the policeman's mind racing.

"O'Doyle?" he repeated, "not *Sean* O'Doyle?"

"Now that you mention it," said Seth, "I think that's what he did say his name was. Big lad – I thought I could trust him," he added, almost to himself.

"Seth did you not hear about the explosion in Gretna earlier this week?"

"I don't read the newspapers," said the carter apologetically. "All that death and destruction all over the place; I'd rather mind me own business, but then something like this happens."

Armstrong felt sorry for the old man on many fronts.

"Seth I think I know what happened to your vehicle. I assume it's the same Sean O'Doyle; if it is, then he worked at the munitions factory at Gretna and he was killed in a massive explosion a couple of days ago. I was told that he owned a vehicle that was destroyed; I saw it myself. Assuming it was the same man, it's also safe to assume it was your vehicle that was lost in the accident."

"Bloody hell!" exclaimed Graham "the poor bugger! He didn't say what he used the van for; he just took it, paid regularly for it and brought it back when he said he would. Poor bugger," he repeated.

"I went round to his lodgings the day before last to check if it was the same man," said Cornelius. "I assumed it was as there was no reply. I intended to re-visit in the next day or two but I think you've just confirmed my suspicions Seth."

*

Inspector Armstrong was troubled by the visit of Seth Graham to the station. Why had Sean O'Doyle hired a motorised vehicle every six weeks seemingly just to go to work? He re-visited the upstairs tenement on Robert Street where he believed O'Doyle stayed; again, the fact that there was no answer reaffirmed his suspicion that O'Doyle was indeed the poor unfortunate. As he was descending the stairs, two women had met at the entrance to the stairwell and were idly chatting to one another. They both simply wore wrap-around smocks and were without coats; one was carrying a bundle of washing, and it was obvious to Armstrong that they also lived in the tenement block.

"Can I disturb you ladies?" Armstrong asked, "I am looking for a man called O'Doyle who lived upstairs, I don't suppose you've seen him recently?"

"Wasn't he one of those two big Irish lads, Vi?" one of the women asked her friend.

"That's right," said Armstrong, "he was Irish."

"Yes him and his friend live across the landing from me," said the woman identified by her friend as Vi. "Two big lads they are both of them. I haven't seen either of them for over a week now."

"Do you know who the landlord is of these properties? Perhaps they would know."

"It could be anybody," replied the other woman, "the co-op had them at one time but they are always sub-contracted out to others. All seems a bit strange if you ask me. I pay *my* rent to some bloke every other Friday – could be anybody."

Armstrong was familiar with the unauthorised practice that he and the authorities had no chance of controlling in this time of war and endless visitors and workers streaming in and out of the city. He thanked the two women with a touch to the brim of his hat and decided on another, rather unorthodox way of finding a little more out about Sean O'Doyle.

*

Wapping may have been an impoverished working class area like many around the city, but as it was due south of the city centre. Reuben Hanks – a native of Caldewgate to the west of the centre – had little business there. But Cornelius Armstrong was aware that his old friend Reuben knew virtually everything that went on amongst the under-classes and if there was some information to be had, then it was almost certain that Reuben would have it.

Armstrong found Hanks in the first place he looked – on a bench at the back of "Blue Lugs" in Caldewgate. He was smoking a clay pipe with his small pug-nosed dog sitting faithfully beside him.

"Hello Reuben," said Cornelius, "I thought I might find you here."

"Hello Mr. Armstrong sir." Hanks was surprised to see the policeman but at the same time he was relaxed as there was no one around who could see him conversing with officialdom. The ears of his little dog pricked up as he recognised the voice of the visitor.

"Hello *Athos*," said Armstrong, patting the dog's head and ruffling his chin. Then turning back to his owner: "I need some information Reuben, about a bloke living in Wapping; I know it's not your usual haunt but you have plenty of connections. He is an Irishman by the name of Sean O'Doyle."

Hanks appeared to physically tense at the mention of O'Doyle's name. "I heard he was killed up at Gretna?"

"That's right," said the inspector, "but there are a few loose ends that I'm looking into. There is talk of another man who stayed at the same place as O'Doyle; as there was another unidentified man killed in the explosion, I'm trying to establish if it is one and the same man."

"It's not," said Hanks instinctively and immediately regretted being so hasty.

"How do you know?" asked Armstrong.

Hanks silently removed his battered flat-topped hat and ran his fingers through his tousled, greasy hair; he then rubbed the stubble on his chin as if stalling for time in order to get his story straight.

Armstrong sensed his hesitancy, "Reuben, if I am to continue to discretely look the other way when I become aware that you are stretching the boundaries of the law, then you need to continue helping me on the odd occasion. Do I make myself clear?"

"Yes Mr. Armstrong," said Hanks resignedly. "O'Doyle stayed with a mate of his called Michael McGinty. McGinty is a giant of a bloke; hard as nails – I think he eats broken glass for breakfast. That said it didn't stop him being hurt recently, and the last I knew he was still in the infirmary. So the other bloke who was killed in the accident couldn't have been McGinty, although I think the two were both usually working at Gretna."

"How did McGinty get hurt?"

Hanks looked sheepish. "Well, as I say, he's a big bloke this McGinty and I heard he was involved in a bare-knuckle contest when he came off second best to an even bigger bloke."

"*You heard?*" asked Armstrong sarcastically, "and did you also *hear* where this fight was?"

"It might have been at the *Golliah* in Wapping. It was brutal, and McGinty was in a real state afterwards. We…I mean…he had to be loaded onto a cart and taken up to hospital – it didn't look as though he was gonna make it he was so badly beaten."

"You seem fairly well-informed for someone who wasn't there," said Cornelius.

The two men looked knowingly at one another.

Visiting the patient

"He is still in a terrible state inspector. He only regained consciousness yesterday. I think it would be better if you came back in a few days' time." The senior nurse was a large officious woman who clearly stood no nonsense from doctors, patients, or as it turned out, policemen. She was known to one and all simply as "Matron."

Cornelius had walked the relatively short distance from his meeting with Reuben Hanks in Caldewgate to the Cumberland Infirmary on Newtown Road, to see Michael McGinty. Whilst appreciating the senior nurse ruled this particular roost, he knew he couldn't afford to waste valuable time given his ever-increasing workload. He looked over the shoulder of Matron into one of the wards behind her: it was full of injured young men; the odd army tunic draped over a chair indicated that they were soldiers, sent back through the clearing stations of Northern France to recuperate in the nearest hospital to their home. This meant most of these men were Border Regiment lads. Cornelius instinctively thought of his cousin George.

Recognising the medical staff's workload was as intense as his own, he had no appetite to get into an argument with Matron but was still keen to see his man, "I can see the pressure you are under," he said, "but I am investigating an explosion at the munitions factory at Gretna on Tuesday night. I believe this man may be able to help."

There was clearly empathy between the over-worked nurse and the policeman, and finally Matron relented. "Very well, I understand. I heard about the explosion – as if we haven't got enough to worry about. I think one or two of the victims were brought here to the morgue. It's bittersweet that although there were fatalities there were no injuries to treat."

"McGinty?" prompted Armstrong.

"Of course, follow me."

As the two walked along the hollow corridors of the hospital, Armstrong noted at least seven wards that were as overcrowded with injured men as the one he had seen at the main entrance. Finally, Matron peeled off left through a double doorway into yet another area that was similarly congested with what Cornelius took to be injured soldiers. He followed the nurse through the ward to the far end where she indicated towards a patient who was lying in the end bed.

"You will need to be gentle with him inspector. He can barely communicate."

"Thank you Matron, I do appreciate this." As she turned to leave him to it, another question occurred to Cornelius, "Before you go," he said "can you tell me if anyone else has visited this man?"

Matron thought for a moment, "I'm pretty sure he hasn't had any visitors. He was brought in on Sunday night and was unconscious until yesterday afternoon." She recalled what the doctor had told her earlier in the week, "Dislocated jaw, fractured cheekbones and eye sockets, broken ribs and internal bleeding. I can't remember the rest."

"Thank you again."

He walked slowly towards the bed. Its occupant could not have been recognised by his closest family. McGinty was propped ever so slightly up with pillows at his back and shoulders. His blackened fingers could just be seen, peeping through dressings on his hand, but it was his head that inevitably drew the attention of anyone who saw him. Swathes of bandages were wrapped tightly and framed a face that was swollen and hideously coloured in black-purple-yellow-green bruising. One eye was completely shut and the other was a slit through which he perceived the presence of a man at his bedside. He was breathing heavily, seemingly with great difficulty.

The man spoke, "Michael McGinty? My name is Armstrong. I'm a policeman."

Although the patient was unable to move or demonstrate any expression, Cornelius sensed that this revelation had created a tension in the injured man. If McGinty had only regained consciousness yesterday and no one else had visited him, then it was obvious to the inspector that he would know nothing of the explosion or the death of his friend. He was therefore cautious about questioning the man too hard and moved to reassure him the best he could, "Don't worry, I am aware of the bare-knuckle contest – that's not the reason I'm here."

This actually caused McGinty even greater distress: *If he's not here about that, there is only one other thing he can be interested in.*

The Irishman mumbled something; the first time he had attempted to speak since coming out of his coma. Armstrong couldn't make it out and leant closer asking him to repeat what he had said.

"How…long…here?" were the barely audible words from the critically ill man.

"How long have you been here?" said Cornelius, seeking to clarify the point, "You've been unconscious for four days."

"Tuesday," McGinty mumbled.

It was clear to Armstrong that he was in no fit state to offer any help with his enquiries regarding the explosion and decided it would be futile to press the man further at this stage, especially when he had no idea about the death of his friend O'Doyle. "I will come back and visit in a couple of days' time," he said.

He left McGinty's bedside and sought out Matron on his way out. "As you suggested," he said, "he is in a bad way."

"Did you get anything out of him?" Matron asked.

"Not really," said Armstrong, "He asked how long he had been in, and mumbled something about Tuesday. Coincidentally that was the night of the explosion – well, early Wednesday morning actually – but I just put it down to incoherent ramblings, having virtually just come round. I will give it a couple of days and then come back and see him when he may be a little more *compos mentis*."

"Is there anything you would like me to do in the meantime?" asked Matron.

"Yes, you can let me know if he has any visitors between now and me returning."

Matron assented to Armstrong's request and the policeman left.

It was now mid-afternoon and Cornelius was already turning his attention to the Friday night ahead. The introduction of the state management scheme had succeeded in easing the nocturnal burden on him and his men, but it had not eradicated the issue of drunkenness and rowdiness entirely. What's more, being the Friday before Christmas – known to everyone as "black-eye Friday" – he knew he was likely to have another busy evening ahead.

*

Earlier that morning, before Inspector Armstrong left to follow up his various lines of enquiry, he had asked one of his men, Sergeant William Smith, to get some background information on the three other young women who were killed in the blast. Smith had always been a bit of a disappointment to Armstrong, who once had high hopes for him as a young constable. But he had not handled his promotion well and his presupposing attitude and often slipshod work meant it was unlikely he would ever progress beyond the rank of sergeant; in fact there had been more than one occasion when he was threatened with *de*-motion, such was the poor quality of his work. But as the substandard police-work of Inspector Godfrey Parker had been tolerated for years, the suggestion of sending Smith back down always smacked of double-standards to his superiors.

Besides, every now and then he would surprise his colleagues with some excellent detective work; and this was one such occasion. Smith had excelled himself and uncovered something that his inspector found extremely interesting upon his return to the station.

Whereas two of the young women were sisters, living local to the factory in Gretna, as Plummer had advised the inspector during his visit the previous day; the third woman originated from Gatehouse of Fleet, where her parents ran

The Ship Inn. When Smith told Armstrong this, the senior man instinctively reached into his pocket and brought out the book of matches he had taken from the unidentified victim's body: the matchbook came from the same pub.

"And there's more," said Smith enthusiastically, "the young lass may be called Amy Flowers now, but her maiden name was Heidelmann – her parents originally being from Germany."

Cornelius never really considered the sabotage theory as being a likely possibility until now. In light of this new information however, and as far- fetched as it seemed, it wasn't completely inconceivable that there had been some form of German infiltration into the biggest munitions factory in the country. Along with the coincidence – if it was coincidence – of an obscure pub in an obscure town cropping up twice, he felt it was well worth his while travelling up to the Galloway Coast to make some more enquiries.

"That's good work Smith," he said at last, "well done."

For the first time Armstrong had that gut-instinct that he was finally making a little headway in the investigation and decided to follow up another line of enquiry with a telegram. He remembered Reuben Hanks told him earlier that McGinty and O'Doyle came from Antrim. Armstrong gave Smith the task of contacting the senior officer at the station there, and seeing if he had any information on Sean O'Doyle.

"If O'Doyle was involved in organising this fight for McGinty," he told his sergeant, "then he wasn't exactly as pure as the driven snow was he?"

Visiting the relatives

The task of visiting bereaved relatives following the death of a loved one was probably the worst duty undertaken by a policeman and a naturally enough, it was one Cornelius Armstrong loathed. Visiting the Lyons to inform them of Katherine's death had been bad enough but given that Elspeth was not a blood relative, it was never going to be as bad as visiting the families of the three other girls who had perished in the blast.

His first visit was to the mother of Morag and Isla Stewart, the two sisters, whose family home was less than a mile and a half from their place of work in Gretna. Armstrong had sent word ahead that he intended to visit but that did not make the task any easier. The pain of Mrs. Stewart was unimaginable as she had lost her husband – the girls' father – in a railway accident some years earlier. She was clearly once an attractive woman but the emotional trauma had taken its toll, and the sagging shoulders and bloodshot eyes gave some clue as to her inner turmoil.

Armstrong felt his own imposition like a dead weight around his shoulders as Mrs. Stewart kindly welcomed him into her home and offered him some tea. He accepted if only to give poor woman something to do in order to momentarily distract her from her agony.

Once they were both seated, Cornelius then attempted to progress his investigation by asking what – even to him – sounded like banal, meaningless questions about the length of times the girls worked at the factory; the job they did; where they worked beforehand; if they knew anyone else in the factory (a question the policeman instantly regretted as soon as he heard himself say it, such was its ridiculous nature); and if they had commented on anything suspicious during their time there.

He was struck by the humility and dignity with which Mrs. Stewart bore her cruel, unimaginable loss. There was a strange juxtaposition of being almost overwhelmed by grief, whilst retaining the presence of mind to act as a courteous host to someone her class recognised as a person of great authority.

The policeman stayed with Mrs. Stewart for around an hour; as much to give her a little company rather than anything else. The injustice suffered by good people sickened him. He left around three o'clock consumed by a feeling of unworthiness and despondency; feelings that were exacerbated by the fact that, as he had suspected prior to his visit, he had learned nothing more than he knew already. He had been a policeman for coming up thirty years, and he was starting to feel tired for the first time; he wondered how long he could take the strain endured in the last couple of years. He wondered if he even wanted to.

As it had been late morning by the time Cornelius had left Carlisle, he knew it would be too late in the day following his visit to Mrs. Stewart to commence the fifty mile journey west to Gatehouse of Fleet, where he wanted to follow up the lead regarding Amy Flowers' German heritage. He had therefore made a reservation at a hotel in Dumfries where he could stay the night and continue on, rather than returning to Carlisle only to head further northwest the following day.

He made the short train journey to Dumfries. Although Amy Flowers hailed from further along the Galloway Coast, she lived in Dumfries with her husband who was serving in France with the Royal Scots. Upon learning of this, Armstrong was instantly reminded of the Quintishill disaster where that regiment suffered such dreadful losses before they even left the country. Wherever Cornelius turned these days, death, destruction and desperation seemed omnipresent.

The detective made some cursory enquiries with neighbours of the young woman; apart from expressing their shock at the accident, no one gave Armstrong cause to believe that Amy was anything other than good and decent. Armstrong returned to his hotel, chose the lightest thing on the menu and decided on an early night.

The other arrangement the inspector had made before leaving Carlisle was to have PC Harry Stokes drive one of the police vehicles up to Dumfries the following day, where he would pick up his superior officer before the two would go on to Gatehouse of Fleet.

"Do you want me to bring someone else, sir?" asked Harry when told of the arrangements, "Joe, perhaps?"

Armstrong thought about the sixty-mile journey back with Joe Brady moaning about everything from the weather to the bumps in the road. "No maybe not," he said, "I'm not expecting any trouble so it should be all right with just the two of us."

Stokes seemed to see through his inspector's veiled excuse and said with a smile, "Very well sir. I expect I shall be up there around eleven o'clock."

*

The night away from home did Cornelius good. By the following morning he had enjoyed a decent night's sleep, cleared his head from the despondency that threatened to overwhelm him after leaving Gretna, and despite facing a similar assignment today – one of visiting bereaved relatives – he felt he had re-discovered his appetite for the investigation. He still wasn't sure if there was a great deal to investigate however; after all no one should be surprised by an explosion in an explosives factory, but his instinct told him that the loose ends that remained were loose enough to merit further enquiry, if only to give some form of understanding to families of the deceased.

As a matter of courtesy he made a quick visit to the Police Station in Dumfries to inform his colleagues of his work that was technically in their patch. He had already left word to that effect prior to leaving Carlisle but wanted to go along and allow them to put a name to a face.

"No problem, inspector," said Jock McGinnis after Cornelius had introduced himself. A big man with a ruddy complexion, McGinnis was the same rank as his Carlisle counterpart and not having been called to the incident in Gretna in the first place, was happy for his colleague to continue the investigation. "If you need any support I could probably spare a man," he added in his broad accent, "but I don't have too many."

"I don't think that will be necessary inspector," said Armstrong, "but I will contact you through the telephone if things change. Before I leave could you just give me the directions to Gatehouse of Fleet?"

"Nay bother," said McGinnis, "if you just head due west towards Stranraer, you'll pass Castle Douglas and Kirkcudbright; Gatehouse is the next decent size town after that. It's an area I know well, coz me dear ol' granny used to stay at Mossyard just beyond it."

The place-name rang a bell with Cornelius, "Mossyard?"

"Aye," said McGinnis, "it's a tiny wee place just beyond Gatehouse. Lovely beaches round that area inspector if you've time for a paddle!"

"Well, as appealing as that sounds, I'm assuming I won't," replied Cornelius with a smile.

The two parted with a handshake and Inspector Armstrong arrived back at his hotel just in time to meet PC Stokes.

"Morning Harry, made good time?" said Armstrong loading his overnight bag into the vehicle.

"Yes, not too bad sir. The roads aren't the greatest round here but at least it's quiet enough." Stokes got out of the driver's seat and pushed his fists into the small of his back, which forced him into an audible straining noise.

"You've put a shift in already, Harry," observed Armstrong, "why don't we have a cup of coffee before we go and I'll take the wheel for the last leg."

When motorised vehicles had been introduced to the city police force at the start of the decade, men of all ranks had been trained in driving.

"That would be much appreciated sir," said Stokes. He was a thirty-year veteran who felt his age on days like these.

The journey westward took a further hour and a half in the functional, if uncomfortable vehicle that did its best to trundle along the uneven roads. The Carlisle men found

Gatehouse to be a sleepy little town that basically consisted of one long street at the base of a gently sloping valley. At the far end of the town was a bridge crossing the Fleet and the first building on the other side was *The Ship Inn*. The hostelry was closed.

Armstrong looked up and down the deserted street: it was a cold winter's afternoon and what he assumed was normally a pretty hideaway seemed to have a depressed feel to it. The smoking chimneys were the only indication that the town was inhabited at all. *No one is exempt from the feeling, not even a place like this,* he thought to himself. He took a deep breath and knocked on the pub door. After a few minutes and couple more encouraging knocks, Cornelius heard the sound of the inner lobby door opening and the main door in front of which he stood, being unbolted.

The door opened to reveal a man who must have been in his sixties and who wore the same desperate expression Armstrong had observed on the face of Mrs. Stewart in Gretna.

With his uniformed colleague standing beside him, it was obvious to anyone what their occupation was but by way of an introduction, Armstrong said it anyway, "Good afternoon sir, my name is Armstrong, I am a policeman."

The man looked nonplussed, "How can I help you?" His accent was clearly foreign.

"Mr. Heidelmann?"

"Yes, I am," he was clearly getting distressed, "I'm sorry, I would prefer if you came back at another time. My wife and I have suffered a great tragedy."

"Yes sir I know," said Armstrong as delicately as he could, "it's about your daughter's death that I'm here."

"I don't understand," said Heidelmann.

"I am investigating the cause of the explosion." Before he could explain further there was an icy blast of wind that whooshed down the street and through the open door of the pub. "Do you mind if we came in for a few minutes?" suggested Cornelius.

Heidelmann reluctantly acquiesced and stood aside to let the two officers in. He bolted the door behind them. "We can go through to the house, where it is a little more comfortable," he said.

He led the two into a sitting room where there was a roaring fire, in front of which sat a woman who was dosing with the heat. Upon her husband entering with the two visitors, she looked up with the same tired eyes that Armstrong was now familiar with. No introductions were necessary.

"I'm sorry to disturb you Mrs. Heidelmann," said Cornelius, "but I need to ask you and your husband some questions about Amy and the factory."

The couple turned out to be as dignified and as hospitable as Mrs. Stewart had been the previous day. Whatever preconceptions Armstrong and his colleagues may have had beforehand about Amy working for her father, who may somehow have been linked to German espionage and saboteurs, could not have been further from the truth.

Diedrich Heidelmann had worked for the German Red Cross in his younger days, while his wife Mary had worked for the British equivalent. The two had met while assisting with the relief effort during the Serbo-Bulgarian War of the mid-1880s. Mary was from Gatehouse and when the two married, Diedrich was more than happy to move to Scotland. This was almost thirty years ago, long before war was ever contemplated with Germany. In the years since, Heidelmann had gone from being welcomed into the town, having married one of its daughters, to becoming fully accepted as part of the close-knit community. He and Mary had owned the *Ship* for over ten years. Amy was their only child. In adulthood she had met and married a young man from Dumfries where they had their home.

Armstrong and Stokes sat in silence as the two – like Mrs. Stewart the previous day – recited their story with great dignity. It was clear that there was no inkling of wrongdoing on the part of the elderly couple but Armstrong needed to ask about one last thing.

He reached into his pocket and brought out the book of matches he had recovered from the unidentified body at the factory. "These matches have the name of your Inn on them," he said, "they were on the body of another victim."

"That is very odd," said Heidelmann, "I am not aware of anyone from Gatehouse working at the factory."

"Besides," continued his wife, "we only took receipt of those matchbooks on Saturday. We received them along with some beer coasters to be used in the bar. They were just a way of advertising the pub. It all seems so pathetic and insignificant now."

"Do you know who could have taken a book?" asked the detective.

Mrs. Heidelmann thought for a while, "I remember Saturday being very quiet; the only person I remember giving a book to, was one of those Irish lads from Mossyard."

Moss Yard? That name again! Armstrong suddenly remembered where he had first heard the name – or read it. He was sure it was on the telegram he found in Katherine Meadows bedroom. "Before we leave," he said, "I noticed you had a telephone as we walked through the bar. I wonder if I could use it please."

"Of course," said Heidelmann tiredly.

Armstrong had the operator connect him with his own police station in Carlisle.

"Bill? It's Armstrong here. Can you remember a few days ago I asked you about Moss Yard – did you have any luck with it?"

Bill Townsend realised he had forgotten to get back to the Inspector on the subject. "Sorry sir, I meant to say, the only thing we could come up with was old Inspector Parker who said his wife's aunt was from up near Castle Douglas and he knew that there was a Mossyard up that way."

"Thank you Bill, that's all I need to know." He returned to the sitting room and asked the Heidelmanns, "Where is this Moss Yard – I thought it was a yard at the back of a street?"

"No – one word," said Mrs Heidelmann , "just a tiny wee place a couple of miles up the road, on the left hand side."

Armstrong thanked the couple, offered his condolences once more and left with PC Stokes. As they climbed back into their vehicle, a van passed them travelling in the opposite direction to which they were facing – it was the only other indication of life the two had seen in their brief visit to Gatehouse. Once back in the vehicle, Cornelius turned to his passenger, "I need to go to this place

200

Mossyard, Harry, in order to satisfy my curiosity once and for all."

Mossyard

Jimmy Heaney was a troubled man. He knew he was under pressure from the War Council to keep the shipments of supplies moving, but without three of his colleagues – and with a fourth completely incapacitated – the effectiveness of the operation was limited. He looked round the large cow shed that was used as a store. There were still enough supplies to last for a few weeks but with him still on crutches after Padraig dropped a crate of stolen rifles on him, breaking his foot and leaving him with only one fit man available, handling the contraband was going to be the problem.

Heaney had informed Belfast of his dilemma as soon as he heard the news from Gretna, but he had received little in the way of sympathy being advised that his colleagues were just "casualties of war" and that he should continue as normal. Heaney decided to send another telegram demanding that at least two men be sent over to him to help. He composed a coded message and instructed his last remaining charge, Connor James, to have it sent, which was slightly awkward as Connor would have to make the ten-mile journey to the telegram office in Kirkcudbright, but Heaney felt he had no choice.

"While you're gone," he said, "I'll go and have a look at that engine on the boat – it's been acting up something terrible of late."

By the time the younger man set off in the van it was mid-afternoon. To get to Kirkcudbright he had to drive through a deserted Gatehouse of Fleet. As he did so he noticed two men – one in uniform – coming out of *The Ship Inn*. He immediately thought of his friend Padraig and their nights at "the Ship." There wasn't much to do round here but they enjoyed a Saturday night there – the most recent one being Saturday gone. Connor remembered commenting to Padraig that it was quieter than usual. "It's the last one you'll ever know my friend," Connor said out loud to himself as he drove on past the pub.

*

Inspector Armstrong and PC Stokes left Gatehouse following the basic directions given by the Heidelmanns – a couple of miles in a westerly direction. Mrs. Heidelmann had told the policemen to keep an eye out as Mossyard could not actually be seen from the road, "It's only a wee place right on the shore with its own little cove," she said, "I think there is a little sign on the roadside but it's not easy to find."

After the approximate distance, Cornelius noticed muddy tire tracks coming from the left and swinging out in front of his vehicle following an easterly direction. This in turn prompted him to slow down and he spotted the sign Mrs. Heidelmann had mentioned, barely visible from behind a lifeless hedge.

"I don't think I would have ever seen that. sir," said Stokes.

"I don't think I would've either Harry, had we not been looking for it. It's certainly secluded, this place."

Armstrong turned onto a dirt track that had been churned up with the winter rain, that didn't appear to have a destination; there was a slight incline for about half a mile that naturally took the eye up to the sea and the horizon beyond. Having no idea where the track was leading, it almost gave Cornelius the impression that he was driving across a causeway.

As they reached the brow of the hill, the track swung to the left and descended towards what appeared from a distance to be little more than three or four buildings. The police vehicle trundled slowly down the hill in a low gear and stopped in front of a large cow shed. Armstrong and Stokes sat momentarily in silence looking around for signs of life. The only sound was the wind moaning across the Solway.

"Seeing as we've made the effort to get here we might as well have a look around," suggested Cornelius. He parked the vehicle to the side of the large shed, sheltering it from the sea wind.

The two policemen wandered over to two cottages diagonally opposite the shed; one had a wisp of smoke coming out its chimney that was instantly snatched away in the wind. Cornelius knocked on the door, not really sure what he was looking for or what he was going to ask the occupant. It made no difference – there was no answer. Harry Stokes rubbed at the window of the dwelling next door and cupped his hand against the glass: nothing.

There was a sandy path that led from the cottages past the opposite side of the barn from where Armstrong parked the police van. It wound its way down towards some trees and presumably on to the cove beyond. Cornelius sensed that Harry was starting to tire after what for him, had already been a long day. He himself didn't really see the point in wandering aimlessly down the path and said, "Presumably those tracks we passed on the roadside were a sign that the owner was leaving on some errand. Maybe we should call it a day."

"Yes, sir," was Harry's relieved reply.

The two walked back towards their vehicle and Cornelius noticed that the large door to the cow shed was slightly open. Out of a policeman's curiosity he instinctively peeked through the crack and gave an almost imperceptible gasp at the sight of a rifle lying on top of a crate. Had it been a shotgun, Armstrong probably wouldn't have given much thought to the matter, being as it was on or near farm land. But the thing that caught his attention was that the rifle was clearly an army-issue Enfield rifle.

"What is it, sir?" asked Stokes, as Armstrong slid the door wide enough for them both to enter.

The inspector didn't need to articulate an answer: inside were dozens of crates, boxes and drums most of which were marked "Property of His Majesty's Government." The crate on which the rifle lay had been pried open and the lid left loose. Armstrong picked up the rifle and lifted the lid to reveal a dozen or more identical weapons.

"Sir?" said Harry, calling his superior's attention to another corner of the shed.

Armstrong followed Stokes's indication towards sacks that were stacked against the wall, away from the other contraband. As the two walked across the distinct smell of cordite became stronger. The sacks on the top of the pile bore the legend "HM Factory Gretna."

Just as the two policemen were trying to comprehend their find, there was a shuffling noise coming from outside the large shed.

*

After Jimmy Heaney had sent Connor on his telegram errand, he had hobbled down to the cove with the aid of a crutch to the small schooner they used for ferrying armaments across the Irish Sea. The engine on the boat had been spluttering and misfiring of late, and Heaney was naturally concerned that one of these days, it would conk out altogether mid-voyage, leaving them to drift helplessly into the arms of the law at which point, their whole operation would be uncovered.

After an hour of hammering and swearing at the smoking engine in the confined space with his restricted mobility, and listening to the wind get louder and feeling the temperature dropping, Heaney finally gave up for the afternoon. "Feckin' thing!" he barked as he threw down a wrench. He picked up his crutch and awkwardly hopped off the boat. The few hundred yards back to the cottage was equally awkward as the crutch continually sank into the soft surface.

He finally made it back but as he was about to enter the cottage he heard a noise coming from the cow shed to his left. He looked across to see the door was open; assuming it was the returning Connor parking the van in the shed he went across to meet him. Upon entering the shed however, he found himself face to face with two men – seeing one was in a police uniform, Heaney knew immediately the game was up.

Armstrong and Stokes similarly knew by the combined look of surprise and guilt on the man's face that they were close to solving the whole case.

Heaney made a futile attempt to turn and run but in his haste he only succeeded in tripping over his crutch and he fell face-first into the muddy track. The two policemen were quickly onto him and Stokes produced some wrist-irons from his belt to secure the man.

Helping him back to his feet and indicating towards the cottage Armstrong said, "Shall we go inside and you can fill in the gaps for us?"

Whatever gaps there were, were destined to be filled virtually without a word being spoken. Inside the cottage were the most basic of amenities but it was to a board in the kitchen area to which Cornelius's attention was instantly drawn. On it were six "Wanted" posters with names printed in a thick black stencil type-face above photographs of the people concerned.

The first one was listed as James "Jimmy" Heaney and the picture was of the man Armstrong had just arrested. The detective glanced across at Heaney, "No doubt rejoicing in your celebrity status and having a good laugh at the expense of the authorities in the process?"

Heaney confirmed Armstrong's suspicion by staying silent and lowering his eyes.

The script below the photograph explained that Heaney was a member of the Ulster Volunteers and was wanted for gun-running and making explosives. The text was repeated for the other five, two of whom – Padraig Byrne and

Connor James – Armstrong had never heard of. The other three were a different matter however. Although he didn't recognise the photographs of the two other men, he recognised their names: Sean O'Doyle and Michael McGinty.

If it was a surprise to Cornelius to see the names of the Irish *men* stuck on an obscure kitchen wall in a remote corner of Scotland, the final poster sent his blood cold. The name was that of Kathleen McSweeny but when he looked at the picture of the young woman, he saw the image of Katherine Meadows looking back at him.

Revelation

Inspector Armstrong made a slow walk across Eden Bridges and up Stanwix Bank towards the Lyons' villa. He walked slowly, not in any great hurry to give more bad news to good, decent people.

It was a pleasant morning and, as on a previous occasion – the morning he first met Katherine Meadows – he found Geoffrey Lyons sitting in his garden.

"Good morning, Geoffrey," he said sombrely; the kind of greeting where the recipient immediately knows that there is something wrong.

"Cornelius!" replied Lyons "is everything all right?" Then, realising the stupidity of his question, added, "Surely things couldn't be any worse than they are?"

"I'm afraid so," said the policeman. Before his host could respond to this cryptic comment he added, "Is Elspeth with you this morning?" Lyons confirmed she was with a silent nod. "Could you ask her to join us please, Geoffrey, I'd like to speak with you both together."

Lyons left Armstrong for a moment and went inside to call his wife. Cornelius meanwhile stood in the beautiful garden taking a moment to appreciate the fresh air, the tweeting of the birds that fluttered around looking for food, and the distant burbling of the River Eden as it meandered its way along, a few hundred yards below. After a few minutes Geoffrey Lyons reappeared with his wife Elspeth; judging by their concerned expressions, he had apparently forewarned her about the impending grave news Cornelius was about to impart.

"Good morning Cornelius," said Elspeth approaching, "whatever is the matter?"

"I have some bad news about your lodger Elspeth, perhaps you should both sit down."

Mrs. Lyons instinctively reached with her left hand for a handkerchief she had discretely tucked in her right sleeve and sat down. "I don't understand," she said, confused, "Katherine was killed in that terrible explosion, wasn't she? How could things be any worse?"

Armstrong breathed heavily through his nose and took one of the other seats at the patio table. "I'm afraid to tell you both that this young woman was someone quite unworthy of your trust." The two looked at him quizzically, prompting him to continue. "Her name was not in fact Katherine Meadows, it was Kathleen McSweeny. She was not a supporter of women's suffrage Elspeth, as she wanted you to believe; she simply used that as a front to disguise her illegal activity, and took advantage of your good nature in the process."

As questions wrestled each other in the minds of Geoffrey and Elspeth, Armstrong allowed a few moments for his revelation to sink in before explaining further. He had succeeded in completing the picture following the arrest of Jimmy Heaney at Mossyard. With the help of two constables from Gatehouse and Kirkcudbright respectively, they had arrested Connor James and returned the two to Carlisle where they confessed to the whole operation in an attempt to get a more lenient sentence.

"The reason she was on the mainland," he continued, "was that she had to flee from Ireland in May 1914 as she was part of the Larne gun-running scandal. She was a member of the Unionist gang tasked with getting arms and munitions into Ireland to supply a group called the Ulster Volunteers, who are opposed to the imposition of Home Rule for Ireland.

"Another member of the gang was Sean O'Doyle. He was Kathleen's sweetheart, and his was the other picture in the locket I found in her room. The two probably couldn't believe their luck when they both found employment at the munitions factory. Once there they developed a fairly fool-proof system that saw them stealing bomb-making materials and hiding it in a remote hamlet on the Galloway Coast before having it smuggled over to Ireland."

"Not entirely fool-proof though?" commented Lyons.

"No," agreed Armstrong. A problem occurred when the third member of the gang – Michael McGinty, who also worked at the factory – was unable to attend for work, when one of the thefts had been arranged."

The inspector went on to tell the two about his original visit to McGinty in hospital; and how, upon his return to Carlisle, he went to see him again. As McGinty was able to communicate a little more the second time, and was now aware of the explosion and Armstrong's uncovering of the smuggling operation, he had revealed the system he and his two friends used to steal the sacks of explosive materials. It could only be done when McSweeny was working in the drying shed and therefore had access to the bags. Her six weekly rotations therefore dictated when the thefts would take place. She would inform O'Doyle of the date and he would order the vehicle from the oblivious carter, Seth Graham.

During the night shift, someone always had to be present in the drying shed, so the girls used to take turns when it came to having their meal-break; three would take it together while one would stay back and keep the machines turning over. McSweeny and her confederates would inevitably organise the thefts to take place on the nights when her colleagues went for their break and she was left alone.

O'Doyle and McGinty worked in the railway hanger adjacent to the drying shed. They would time their meal-break to coincide with McSweeny being left on her own and the three would secrete one or two sacks into the hired vehicle O'Doyle parked in the shadows at the back of the hanger. The advantage of taking small amounts little and often was twofold: such amounts wouldn't arouse suspicion, given that hundreds of thousands of tons that were produced each week; and secondly, such a theft wouldn't take a great deal of time or effort to load one or two bags to the vehicle, so it would be unlikely they would be seen or missed from where they were supposed to be.

O'Doyle would then casually cover the bags up with a tarpaulin and drive off after his shift was completed, as bold as brass. But instead of heading back to his digs in Carlisle, he would drive up to the tiny hamlet of Mossyard, beyond Kirkcudbright on the Galloway Coast where another gang was storing the stolen goods and more besides. The location was perfect as it was an isolated farm over a mile from the main road with its own bay where the munitions could be distributed, either across to Ireland or to other parts of the mainland. The stash was coordinated by another Irishman, James Heaney.

The plan had run smoothly for over six months until McGinty was incapacitated due to the bare-knuckle fight at the *Golliah*. As Heaney was under pressure to provide more bomb-making materials he instructed O'Doyle to go ahead with the theft as planned and provided one of his own men, Padraig Byrne, to take the place of McGinty. Byrne would meet O'Doyle at Eastriggs before his shift and hide in the back of the vehicle while Sean drove into the compound. He would then appear from the shadows at the appointed time and help O'Doyle lift the heavyweight sacks onto the van.

Inspector Armstrong concluded his narrative, "I can only assume that the system employed by the three gang members was somehow compromised by the new man Byrne, with catastrophic results."

"And the other victims?" asked Elspeth.

"Perhaps that's the biggest tragedy of all," said Cornelius, "they must have been returning from their meal break and were caught in the blast – completely innocent of any wrongdoing."

Elspeth broke into a fit of uncontrollable sobbing.

As he comforted his wife, Geoffrey Lyons asked, "What led you to this incredible outcome?"

Inspector Armstrong explained, "Although I didn't know it at the time, the first clues were the locket and the telegram I found in McSweeny's room. The telegram made reference to a Padraig from Mossyard. Then there was the fact that there was an unidentified body in the explosion, which turned out to be this Padraig incidentally; added to that was the fact that McGinty should have been there but wasn't and poor old Seth Graham's vehicle had been hired but not returned. I suppose it was all of these little loose ends that in a roundabout way eventually led me to the arms dump in Scotland. Once we found that and arrested Heaney, it all fell into place.

"When I returned to Carlisle I checked McSweeny and O'Doyle's images against those in the locket we thought belonged to a Katherine Meadows – they had even the bare faced effrontery to use the photographs from the "Wanted" posters and reproduced them in tiny form to insert them in the locket."

"That's why neither was smiling in their respective picture," said Lyons.

"Precisely," said Cornelius, "no doubt McSweeny found that highly amusing, as they all did by displaying their respective posters at the cottage at Mossyard."

"How did they acquire so much?" asked Geoffrey.

"Now there's a question!" replied the policeman. "Upon questioning Heaney it transpires there are these little three-man – or sometimes woman – gangs working throughout the north of England and Scotland. They are constantly working to steal weaponry of any kind and funnel them through to Mossyard where it is distributed accordingly to facilitate the radicals' illegal activity. We also found armaments there that had been stolen from military bases at Berwick, Edinburgh and even here in Carlisle.

"I can only conclude in this time of war, when tens of thousands of men and women are constantly on the move and the transportation of arms and ammunition is an everyday feature, it is relatively straightforward for these gangs to keep their own shadow trade moving. Being such small numbers and stealing little and often appears to be the key to their success; if one group is infiltrated it doesn't necessarily disrupt the rest of the operation – or perhaps I should say, industry."

"Well if you haven't completely eradicated the problem nationally, Cornelius, you have certainly solved the problem locally, with the discovery of the hoard in Scotland."

"Yes," agreed the inspector with an air of resignation, "We are in the process of alerting the authorities near the other munitions factories and armaments depots around the country, which is no small task.

"Of course, sadly that won't bring back those poor innocent girls who will no doubt be simply marked down as yet more needless loss during these cruel times."

The best laid plans

The first cordite had been produced as early as August 1916, less than eighteen months since the commencement of the building of the factory. The timing of the announcement of the Gretna factory could not have been better for Sean O'Doyle, Kathleen McSweeny and Michael McGinty.

The three had joined the Ulster Volunteers, who were opposed to the government's Home Rule Bill in Ireland, at its inception in 1912. With McSweeny's guile, O'Doyle's charm and McGinty's sheer brute strength, they had proven themselves an effective gang and had played a key part in the Larne gun-running incident in April 1914, with McSweeny even travelling to Germany as part of the planning for the operation.

Following the outbreak of the war, Edward Carson himself, founder of the loyalist paramilitary group, had requested the three be stationed on the mainland, where they could be used to identify and purloin arms and munitions during the confusion of war. It was straightforward enough for the men to blend in as two Irish workers among the thousands of navvies working up and down the country. McSweeny however needed a more delicate approach and she found it through the Women's Suffrage Movement.

One of the key elements of any successful nefarious group is to adopt subtle machinations that see them infiltrate the most seemingly innocent, vulnerable group for their own wicked ends. Such was the case with the Ulster Volunteers who through an intricate web had established connections with the unsuspecting Irish Women's Suffrage Society. It was fairly straightforward therefore to concoct a virtuous back story for McSweeny and secure her a place within the society. As the group had strong links with Millicent Fawcett's National Union of Women's Suffrage Societies on the mainland, Kathleen McSweeny made the short crossing to Liverpool and bided her time.

That time came when she met Elspeth Lyons, chairwoman of the Cumberland Suffrage Society at a rally in Manchester. It wasn't long before she had curried sufficient favour with Elspeth to move in with her and her husband Geoffrey under the pretext of looking for work in the area.

Once Lloyd George made the announcement of a munitions factory being built on the Scottish border, O'Doyle, McGinty and McSweeny were all in the prime position to take full advantage. The two men first secured jobs helping build the factory and the surrounding townships, and were then taken on once production started. Equally Kathleen – upon her return to Carlisle from Manchester – had little trouble securing a position in the factory that was destined to be dominated by female workers whose job it would be to provide materials for the male counterparts in mainland Europe.

It had only taken O'Doyle and McSweeny a matter of weeks to establish a way of stealing sacks of cordite from the factory and transporting them up to Mossyard.

O'Doyle knew the rag and bone man Gilly Millholme, who also lived in Wapping, after meeting him one night in *The Golliah*. In the course of a conversation about his cart, Gilly told O'Doyle about the carter Seth Graham who had a motor vehicle. O'Doyle made arrangements to hire the vehicle from Seth on a regular basis, knowing that his girlfriend, Kathleen McSweeny, worked in the drying shed at six-week intervals. McSweeny meanwhile arranged the on-shift rotas between her and her unsuspecting colleagues to have a half-hour spell on each shift where she would be on her own. Once all of the constituent parts were in place O'Doyle, McGinty and McSweeny put their operation into effect with stunning results. For a few months, their plan worked like clockwork; that was until O'Doyle and McGinty's greedy oversight that took the bigger man out of the equation.

With McGinty in hospital fighting for his life, Sean met with Kathleen knowing that he was under pressure to deliver more cordite to Mossyard but without the brute strength of his friend to help him it would prove extremely difficult; with the best will in the world, he knew there was no way he could lift the heavy sacks up onto the van himself, even with Kathleen's help.

Kathleen advised him to contact Jimmy Heaney at the arms store and see if they could cancel the forthcoming weeks' theft. O'Doyle did as McSweeny suggested but was given short shrift by Heaney who offered to send one of his own men – Padraig Byrne – to help with the lifting instead. O'Doyle would meet Byrne at Eastriggs before his shift began and Byrne would hide in the back of the hired vehicle in order to sneak into the compound and wait until the appointed hour. Having visited the store at Mossyard many times O'Doyle not only knew Heaney but his two men Byrne and Connor James. Amongst the people that knew him, Byrne was not renowned for his witty repartee and pearls of wisdom. But as he was required for his muscles and not his brainpower, Sean accepted Heaney's instruction without any protest, mindful that it was essentially his own greed that led to McGinty being incapacitated. He duly sent Kathleen a telegram advising her of Heaney's instructions and arranged to meet her in the usual place, at the usual time, the following Tuesday night.

*

Kathleen McSweeny, under the guise of Katherine Meadows, accepted her lot pragmatically and went about her business. Living a lie in the home of Elspeth Lyons, attending suffrage meetings she had little interest in, and working shifts at HM Gretna was all for a greater good: supporting the man she loved and ultimately, keeping Ireland as part of the Union.

Being a bright woman with an aptitude for most things, and an ability to pick up a new job with the minimal amount of training, she was one of the few girls who were moved between plants doing various jobs as part of a regular shift pattern. It was a role that Kathleen had effectively engineered for herself, with the main goal of getting to work in the drying section where the cordite went through its final process. From there, the large sacks of explosive mixture would be shuttled to the vast brick warehouses beside the main railway line at Mossband, on the south side of the border, in preparation for distribution to shell-filling factories around the country. It was considered the most dangerous area of the factory, with the possibility of fire caused by the vapours of the drying material, a very real danger. It was a risk McSweeny and her confederates were more than willing to take however.

O'Doyle and McGinty were based in the railway shed beside the drying section, from where they maintained the miles and miles of track around the factory upon which endless bags and drums of explosive-making materials were transported between processes. It was a perfect job for the two navvies – and many hundreds like them – who had spent years on the mainline building railways up and down the country.

It was during the night shifts that McSweeny worked in the drying shed when she, O'Doyle and McGinty would arrange to be separate from their respective colleagues and secrete an amount of cordite in the back of Seth Graham's hired vehicle. Kathleen would then return via train to Carlisle after her shift, while Sean and Michael would drive up to Mossyard to supplement Jimmy Heaney's mini arsenal.

On this particular night, as long as Sean could smuggle Padraig Byrne into the factory grounds, he and McSweeny didn't anticipate any alteration to their tried and trusted method of theft. Heaney had briefed Byrne on what was required, and when O'Doyle picked Padraig up at the *The Graham Arms* in Eastriggs just before nine o'clock, he himself reiterated what was required.

"No problem Sean," said Padraig, in such a broad Irish accent, it even made O'Doyle smile to himself, "no problem at all. You just go about your business and I'll be as quiet as a church mouse in the back of the van. As long as yer man doesn't lift the sheet up when we go in it should be fine."

"It'll be a long wait mind you," O'Doyle told his man, "Kathleen normally sends the other girls for their break around two o'clock."

"No problem Sean, no problem at all. I'll just have myself a little kip until you give me a knock when you need me."

The plan worked well with Sean showing his pass at the gate, all the while, Padraig remained unseen and unsuspected under the tarpaulin sheet. He drove a mile or so to his place of work and parked the hired vehicle in the shadow of the giant railway shed and immediately beside a narrow gauge track that led from the drying shed to the distribution warehouses. Intermittently, throughout his shift, O'Doyle stole away from his work to discretely check on Byrne only to find him snoring lightly each time.

Finally, the time came. Sean's colleagues left their stations on the stroke of two o'clock went to the rear of the giant shed where they had their tea and sandwiches. O'Doyle made some excuse meanwhile and told the lads he would join them shortly. He returned to his vehicle and shook Padraig. As he did so, he looked across at the entrance to the equally large drying shed and saw Kathleen waving in the darkness that was only interrupted by soft beams of light emanating from the security lamps that randomly peppered the site.

"Padraig," O'Doyle hissed, "*Padraig*, wake up ye buck eejit!"

"*Uh!* Oh, is it time Sean?" said Byrne instinctively reaching in his pocket for a roll up.

"*What are you doing?*" scolded O'Doyle, "you don't smoke round here. You'll blow the lot of us up man."

"Oh, right Sean, yes. I never thought."

221

"Well just make sure to you do think. Now come on Kathleen is ready for us."

While O'Doyle had been laying down the law, McSweeny had disappeared back inside to prepare for the larceny. She had earmarked two sacks for her stronger male colleagues to manhandle onto one of the small trolley bogies that would enable them to be wheeled out to the vehicle without causing undue noise or disruption. Ordinarily, even if the well-known O'Doyle and McGinty were seen in or around the drying shed, it would be assumed that they would be there to fix some element of the transport equipment. If they were discovered in the act of wheeling sacks over to the vehicle, it would be assumed that they were simply transporting the load to the distribution warehouses. This night carried a little more of a risk given that no one knew Byrne, but as long as the three acted quickly, there shouldn't be a problem.

O'Doyle and Byrne scampered across the open ground between the two buildings and entered the drying shed.

"Jaysus and g'way!" exclaimed Padraig, struck by the awesome interior, "would ch'look at the size of this place!" Like every new visitor, he was struck by the overpowering vapours coming from the mixture. There must have been twenty large stoves lined up at fifty-yard intervals, each serviced by teams of four girls. Byrne could hear activity at the far end of the workhouse, several hundred yards away, but this end was relatively quiet, with most of the girls seemingly on their break. The cordite was spread out on large trays where the solvents were being drawn off. "Tis an amazing sight to be sure!" said Padraig in his wonderment.

"Never mind that," instructed O'Doyle, "give me a hand with these sacks. Almost forgetting himself he turned to Kathleen whom he hadn't seen for over a week, and gave her a peck on the cheek, "Hello, sweetheart you're doing a grand job."

"I've missed you Sean," she said simply.

"I've missed you too, sweetheart." Concerned at the possibility of unnecessary delays O'Doyle set about loading the sacks on to one of the small bogie trolleys.

Sean and Padraig wheeled the trolley along the line as the enormous factory went about its business, ignorant of any wrongdoing. Once in the shadows behind the railway shed the two men brought the bogie to a silent halt and heaved the sacks as noiselessly as possible onto the back of the vehicle.

"At least I'll have a comfy mattress for the rest of the night," said Byrne.

O'Doyle wasn't particularly amused, "Let's just get this tarpaulin back over I'll wheel this bogie back across to the drying shed."

Padraig was aware that Kathleen had followed the two of them across the open space between the two buildings and made an alternative suggestion, "No I'll take it Sean. I don't doubt you two young'uns want to do a bit of canoodling."

Sean and Kathleen looked at one another and smiled, not having seen each other for so long. "Very well," agreed O'Doyle, "but be quick about it and then get back out of sight."

"Yes, the girls will be back soon," added McSweeny.

Padraig wheeled the bogie back along the line and into the drying shed making sure he left it in the same place. Upon re-entering the shed he was again struck by the almost overwhelming odour permeating from the numerous trays of drying mixture. As he turned to leave, the yellow stains on the rim of one of the large stoves caught his eye. His natural curiosity took him over to it; running his finger along the rim he put it to his nose and snapped his head back in protest. Although he was used to handling the material, it was never in this raw state. Laughing at his own stupidity, his eye moved to some of the trays and his mind started to picture how the process worked. In his absentmindedness, while stooping low to see back inside the stove, he instinctively reached in his inside pocket for a roll-up. He struck a match, lit the cigarette and slipped the match-book back into his pocket. As he did so he heard a voice behind him.

"Who are you?"

He turned to see three young women walking towards him; like Kathleen they were all dressed in boiler suits, rubber-soled shoes and bonnets.

One then exclaimed in horror, *"He's lit a cigarette!"*

The third shouted, *"You can't smoke in ..."* but she never completed the sentence.

The lingering vapours caught hold of the naked flame and the air immediately whooshed into a flash fire.

Outside, Sean and Kathleen had only been talking for less than a minute when they heard a scream coming from the drying shed.

"What's that feckin' eejit done now?" growled O'Doyle, breaking into a run. He and Kathleen sprinted towards the entrance of the shed but were destined never to make it.

Historical note

The brief history of Woodrow Wilson and his family as recounted in *The Young American* is essentially accurate. Whereas much artistic licence has been afforded to his two visits to the city as described in this volume, the fact that he visited Carlisle during the summer of 1896 and then again as President in December 1918 is truthful.

The first was part of his cycling tour of the Lakes when he was a professor at Princeton University. His neighbour Mrs. Brown is known to have paid for the trip as part of Wilson's recuperation, following a mild stroke in May 1896. Staying at the Central Plaza Hotel (not the Station Hotel as described), Wilson spent a few days in the city before embarking on his cycling tour. So enamoured was he with the Lakes, he is known to have made at least a further three visits to the Lake District.

He was inaugurated President of the United States in March 1913 and was re-elected for a second term in November 1916. His second visit to Carlisle was as described: what he called his "pilgrimage of the heart," as he was in Europe to visit the King and Queen in London, and attend the peace conference in Paris.

Whereas Woodrow Wilson was very real, Jacob Turn and his brother John Henry were not. There are reports of body snatching incidents in connection with St. Cuthbert's Church and Stanwix Cemetery in the early nineteenth century, but the city's main association with the despicable crime was the known fact that William Hare resided there following his fleeing Edinburgh, after the hanging of his partner in crime, William Burke.

His Majesty's Factory, Gretna, was the country's largest cordite factory during World War I and, as described, was one of over two hundred throughout the country built in direct response to the Shell Crisis of 1915.

More than twenty thousand workers, mostly women, were employed at the factory, and at its peak it produced 800 tons of cordite per week. The mixture was christened "The Devil's Porridge," by Sir Arthur Conan Doyle who visited the factory in 1917 and witnessed the nitro glycerine being mixed with the gun-cotton to make the cordite.

The physical and psychological demands on the female workers were considerable. Their skin turned yellow with the sulphur – giving them the nickname "the canary girls" – and many experienced teeth falling out and brittle bones due to their exposure to the toxic chemicals. Fire posed serious risks especially for those working in the drying section. Many explosions are known to have occurred at the factory during the war years and at least three people are known to have died as a result.

As described in this volume, drunkenness in Carlisle peaked in 1916, due to the thousands of workers, with more than 900 convictions being recorded. To address the problem, the government considered prohibition but eventually decided on an experiment originally developed in Gothenburg, Sweden, where similar problems had been experienced.

The state management scheme, or the "Carlisle Experiment" as the government termed it was therefore introduced in 1916 to control the selling and consumption of alcohol. It was only supposed to run for the duration of the war and twelve months thereafter. In reality it carried on for more than fifty years and turned out to be the longest experiment in British political history.

Much of the second case in this volume takes place in an area of the city known as Wapping, which – unlike the more familiar wards of Caldewgate and Shaddongate – may be unfamiliar to many modern-day Carliseans, as the name is no longer used. It was (or is) the area immediately to the southwest of the city centre, essentially beginning at the top of James Street. Back in the day, it then incorporated the whole of the area between Botchergate to the east and the River Caldew to the west, and continued south before meeting Currock, a ward that is still familiar to locals today.

In these early decades of the twenty-first century, the area has a few small industrial and retail parks but up until the mid-twentieth century it was a heavily populated area with rows of houses and tenements – that were homes to hundreds of families – and had dozens of shops, a school and a church, factories and breweries. The only discernible link between then and now is James Street, which still has the Victorian Baths on one side and the Metal Box factory (originally Hudson Scott & Sons – the lithographers and decorated sheet metal box manufacturers) on the other.

Finally, I should point out that any dialogue, attributed to real people, in this volume is of my own creation.

Martin Daley

Martin Daley
The Casebook of Inspector Armstrong Volume IV

Detective Inspector Cornelius Armstrong will return in the fourth volume of his casebook.

In *The Roman Mask*, Carlisle's two-thousand-year-old history is brought into sharp focus after a rare artefact is stolen from an auction house in London. When it is rumoured that the relic has found its way to the city that was once the furthest northern outpost of the Roman Empire, Inspector Armstrong is called to investigate. His inquiries lead him in an unexpected direction but will they lead to the recovery of the valuable antiquity?

The second case in the volume develops after Cornelius is casually introduced to a young man by a mutual acquaintance. This chance meeting coincides with a series of seemingly unconnected events that gradually combine and lead the detective to *The Twelve Men*.

Also from MX Publishing

MX Publishing is the world's largest specialist Sherlock Holmes publisher, with over a hundred titles and fifty authors creating the latest in Sherlock Holmes fiction and non-fiction.

From traditional short stories and novels to travel guides and quiz books, MX Publishing cater for all Holmes fans.

The collection includes leading titles such as *Benedict Cumberbatch In Transition* and *The Norwood Author* which won the 2011 Howlett Award (Sherlock Holmes Book of the Year).

MX Publishing also has one of the largest communities of Holmes fans on Facebook with regular contributions from dozens of authors.

www.mxpublishing.com

Also from MX Publishing

Our bestselling books are our short story collections;

'Lost Stories of Sherlock Holmes' , 'The Outstanding Mysteries of Sherlock Holmes', The Papers of Sherlock Holmes Volume 1 and 2, 'Untold Adventures of Sherlock Holmes' (and the sequel 'Studies in Legacy) and 'Sherlock Holmes in Pursuit', 'The Cotswold Werewolf and Other Stories of Sherlock Holmes' – and many more......

www.mxpublishing.com

Also from MX Publishing

The Missing Authors Series

Sherlock Holmes and The Adventure of The Grinning Cat
Sherlock Holmes and The Nautilus Adventure
Sherlock Holmes and The Round Table Adventure

"Joseph Svec, III is brilliant in entwining two endearing and enduring classics of literature, blending the factual with the fantastical; the playful with the pensive; and the mischievous with the mysterious. We shall, all of us young and old, benefit with a cup of tea, a tranquil afternoon, and a copy of Sherlock Holmes, The Adventure of the Grinning Cat."
Amador County Holmes Hounds Sherlockian Society

Also from MX Publishing

The Detective and The Woman Series

The Detective and The Woman

The Detective, The Woman and The Winking Tree

The Detective, The Woman and The Silent Hive

"The book is entertaining, puzzling and a lot of fun. I believe the author has hit on the only type of long-term relationship possible for Sherlock Holmes and Irene Adler. The details of the narrative only add force to the romantic defects we expect in both of them and their growth and development are truly marvelous to watch. This is not a love story. Instead, it is a coming-of-age tale starring two of our favorite characters."

Philip K Jones

www.mxpublishing.com

Also from MX Publishing

The Sherlock Holmes and Enoch Hale Series

The Amateur Executioner

The Poisoned Penman

The Egyptian Curse

"The Amateur Executioner: Enoch Hale Meets Sherlock Holmes", the first collaboration between Dan Andriacco and Kieran McMullen, concerns the possibility of a Fenian attack in London. Hale, a native Bostonian, is a reporter for London's Central News Syndicate - where, in 1920, Horace Harker is still a familiar figure, though far from revered. "The Amateur Executioner" takes us into an ambiguous and murky world where right and wrong aren't always distinguishable. I look forward to reading more about Enoch Hale."

Sherlock Holmes Society of London

www.mxpublishing.com

Also from MX Publishing

When the papal apartments are burgled in 1901, Sherlock Holmes is summoned to Rome by Pope Leo XII. After learning from the pontiff that several priceless cameos that could prove compromising to the church, and perhaps determine the future of the newly unified Italy, have been stolen, Holmes is asked to recover them. In a parallel story, Michelangelo, the toast of Rome in 1501 after the unveiling of his Pieta, is commissioned by Pope Alexander VI, the last of the Borgia pontiffs, with creating the cameos that will bedevil Holmes and the papacy four centuries later. For fans of Conan Doyle's immortal detective, the game is always afoot. However, the great detective has never encountered an adversary quite like the one with whom he crosses swords in "The Vatican Cameos."

"An extravagantly imagined and beautifully written Holmes story"
   (**Lee Child**, NY Times Bestseller, Jack Reacher series)